"You must undress," he said

Ji Yue recoiled in shock, her heart beating triple time. It was one thing to be the woman caressing Bo Tao, bringing him to a place where he had no control over his body. It was quite another to remove her own attire.

"If you wish to know how to seduce a man," Bo Tao said softly. "It begins with your body. And your body is very beautiful to me, Ji Yue." She saw honesty in his eyes, and her heart broke. How had she come to this?

But if her future was in a harem—many women to one man—she would take whatever memories she could. So she put her hands on her buttons and began to pull off her clothes.

"No. Not like you are at a dressmaker's," he said. "Slowly, shyly. But with a hunger in your eyes."

As a virgin, she should not know what he meant, but she felt a longing and a building excitement in what she did. And in what they risked together. She looked at him, letting him see her desire, her fears and her desperate wish....

"My heaven..." he murmured. And if she doubted the desire in his voice, all she had to do was look down. His jade stem was making an appearance....

Blaze

Dear Reader,

Imagine my surprise when I discovered that network television did *not* invent contests for finding a mate. I mean, sure, there was Cinderella, but that was just a fairy tale. Who knew that in 1851 the Emperor of China truly did advertise for all the eligible young women in the land to apply to become his new empress? Of course, he wasn't looking for just one wife. One lucky winner would become his empress, four became primary concubines and then he had two levels of harems below that for when he got bored. Lucky him! And lucky me, too, because I got to explore all the drama, the fear and the excitement vicariously through my heroine.

Now, I'll be the first to admit that I had to change certain historical facts to make it more dramatic. If you're curious, I've put a brief article up on my Web site about the changes I've made. Check it out at www.jadeleeauthor.com. But don't let reality spoil your fun!

Step now into the sensuous, exotic world of China's Forbidden City, where the women are beautiful, the men are usually cut and the emperor rules over everything with absolute power. Then see if you can pick the winner in a game of power and love!

Enjoy!

Jade Lee
www.jadeleeauthor.com

Jade Lee

THE CONCUBINE

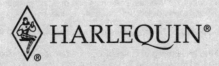

HARLEQUIN®

TORONTO • NEW YORK • LONDON
AMSTERDAM • PARIS • SYDNEY • HAMBURG
STOCKHOLM • ATHENS • TOKYO • MILAN • MADRID
PRAGUE • WARSAW • BUDAPEST • AUCKLAND

Recycling programs
for this product may
not exist in your area.

ISBN-13: 978-0-373-79453-9
ISBN-10:   0-373-79453-3

THE CONCUBINE

Copyright © 2009 by Katherine Grill.

This edition published by arrangement with Harlequin Books S.A.

www.eHarlequin.com

Printed in U.S.A.

ABOUT THE AUTHOR

Children of mixed races have their own set of rules. As the daughter of a Shanghai native and a staunch Indiana Hoosier, *USA TODAY* bestselling author Jade Lee struggled to find her own identity somewhere between the U.S.A. and China. In the end, she found her answers in writing fiction about the amazing power of love.

Books by Jade Lee

HARLEQUIN BLAZE
374—THE TAO OF SEX

Thank you, Brenda, editor extraordinaire, for inviting me to explore the sexuality of China.

I had so much fun with this, I feel like I won something way better than the title of Empress!

Prologue

1851—Imperial China

A LAND OF SENSUOUS DELIGHTS and grinding poverty. A land of silk and jade, of tiny feet and dark, exotic eyes. The ruler of this vast and opulent land is the newly appointed Emperor Xian Feng, the Son of Heaven. Only nineteen years old, he has inherited a corrupt bureaucracy, the rebellious Taiping of the northwest, and a country slowly losing its mind to opium. The eunuchs who serve him grow more corrupt. The white devils constantly bang on his doors demanding trade for goods he does not want. And yet in all this his first duty is to sire an heir. In fact, he will not receive his full imperial salary until he has the required twenty-eight wives.

To this end, the Festival of Fertility has been declared! Eligible women from throughout the land have been invited to come to the Forbidden City, Xian Feng's home in Peking. Their virtue and their fortunes will be examined, they will be tested for lucky aspects of mind and body, and if successful, they will never leave the Forbidden City again. The winner will become the empress herself. Second place goes to four favored concubines. Then two other harems will be established for women who will likely never grace Xian Feng's bed.

A daunting task for any man to oversee, especially one who

is simultaneously running a country. And so, in this most difficult hour, Xian Feng turns to his childhood friend and names
Sun Bo Tao, former bad boy of the Forbidden City, as master
of the festival. Apparently, the emperor does not hear the
warnings that he is appointing a fox to run an imperial henhouse.

1

SUN BO TAO GROANED as his bed dropped to the street with a head-splitting thump. He cursed under his breath even as he wondered why he was dreaming about sleeping in the middle of a noisy Peking street. Then the sharp bark of command from a soldier cut through his dream and jerked him upright. Unfortunately, it didn't change his bizarre surroundings. His bed was still sitting in the middle of a Peking street. He could hear the cry of a hundred hawkers, and the smell of human waste was unmistakable.

He yawned wide enough to crack his jaw, the sound bringing enough awareness that he had to fully open his eyes. He was in a red silk bower surrounded by cushions and hidden from view by tattered silk curtains. Oh, yes, he was sitting in an imperial palanquin and not one of the better ones. He'd woken as the porters dropped the bower onto the city street. But why was he here instead of in his own carriage?

A memory teased at the corners of his mind, but he resolutely pushed it away. There was a reason he had drunk himself into a stupor last night, and he was fairly certain he didn't want to remember what it was. He did recall that he'd been on his way home—walking because he'd been too drunk to ride his horse—when he'd seen the imperial procession. Two soldiers in front of four porters carried a curtained bower through the city streets. A very small procession. It was headed somewhere in Peking—he didn't care where—then would eventually wend its way back to the Forbidden City. As that was his destination, he'd waved down the lead soldier, paid the bribe and slipped in while the porters were taking a rest break. This way he'd get a few more hours of sleep before he had to face the day.

He was just lying back down when a female wail cut through the relative peace of his secluded bower. And worse, it was quickly followed by more feminine screeching. Much as he tried to block out the sound, curiosity drew him out of sleep. Just how many women were wailing loud enough to wake their ancestors?

There was an annoying tear in the curtains. The sunlight streamed through it enough that he could peer out. But did he really want to know what was out there? Yes, apparently his curiosity was in full force today. So with a heavy sigh, he maneuvered himself to the side to look out. Roof tiles. He saw roof tiles first. Broken ones that clearly indicated he sat in a not-so-prosperous area of Peking. But he saw trees, too, and a songbird cage beside a long front wall. Not-so-poor, either, then. Middling aristocracy. He shifted up to his knees to adjust his view.

The father appeared first. Pinched face, short nose, but with a scholarly demeanor. There was refinement in his motions and a kind of tired dreaminess that confirmed Bo Tao's first thought: middling aristocracy. Probably a Manchu of the red banner tribe. Sure enough, he saw a brand-new silk banner on the archway, but that was the only new decoration. The rest of the house was falling into ruin. His gaze returned to the father, then moved lower still to a pair of silent prepubescent boys. The family would have great difficulty finding the money to educate those two.

Bo Tao yawned again and thought to lie back down. But as he shifted, he caught sight of the women. It was the mother who was making the primary racket, weeping and sobbing as only a woman could. It was all for show as she kissed her daughter goodbye. He counted ten paid wailers howling in the background, pulling at their hair and creating a solid wall of sound.

Was the palanquin for them? Were the porters supposed to pick up someone before returning to the Forbidden City? Not the mother, who was still wailing like a demon. Not the stoic father or too-young boys. Must be the girl. He narrowed his eyes, trying to get a look at the daughter. She appeared the right age for marriage, was of middling stature and certainly dressed in finery. He saw an embroidered gown and a curtain of ivory beads in front of her face. Ivory, not jade. Which meant she was not wealthy enough to become an imperial consort.

Ox piss! Now he remembered why he had drunk himself insensate yesterday. The Festival of Fertility commenced this morning. Yi Zhen, his double-damned best friend (now called Emperor Xian Feng, the pompous prick), had just finished mourning his father last night. Which meant he now began the royal process of picking wives and harems in order to beget the next Son of Heaven.

A full week would be given over to the search for beautiful and fertile women to grace Emperor Xian Feng's bed. Beauty and bribes, sex and petty backstabbing would rule the Forbidden City for at least a week, and not a single moment would be left for the practical matters of running the country. What a total waste of time!

Worse, a delegation of Dutch were coming to the Forbidden City this week. Bo Tao believed that the whites had to be handled with great care, that the world had many dangerous powers that were unknown in China. But Yi Zhen was overwhelmed with internal matters, with the Taiping rebellion in the northwest and China's increasingly corrupt infrastructure. He had no time to discuss Dutch delegates and no patience for his best friend, who warned of yet more struggles on a global stage.

Bo Tao should have left the Forbidden City as soon as his emperor showed signs of strain. He knew Yi Zhen's moods, and yet he had not been able to resist pushing his emperor to see the larger picture. That had been his last, most stupid mistake. After all, Bo Tao had no official status. He was merely the hellion of the Forbidden City, the boy who'd run wild with the emperor, playing games throughout the city-within-a-city. If he were an official appointee, if he were a general or a scholar or something with a title, then he might have had the status to force his friend to listen. But he was simply a consultant, a friend to the emperor, a man who saw the greed in the whites' eyes and feared it. And when he had pushed Yi Zhen to see it as well, his best friend had punished him.

His triple-damned emperor had named Bo Tao master of the festival! He said Bo Tao had become too serious and needed a week of frivolity to lighten his mood. Ox piss! Yi Zhen was merely flexing his royal muscles! Rather than deal with the coming Dutch delegation, Yi Zhen had ignored the issue, ordered Bo Tao to take care of the festival, and then laughed at his friend's stunned expression. It was just like when they were children! Whenever Yi Zhen had felt threatened, he would reassert his status as a royal prince. He'd usually make up some crime and have the eunuchs punish Bo Tao. That was how Bo Tao had learned the fine art of scrubbing kitchen pots or worse, cleaning chamber pots.

This was no different. But instead of a game, Bo Tao was

suddenly in charge of scores of competitive, backstabbing, gossiping virgins! Just when the Dutch delegation was due to arrive!

He glared out the torn curtain at the girl who might very well become one of his charges by the end of the day. Narrowing his eyes, he tried to assess her prospects and understand why she was marked as special. She had to have something unique to rank an imperial palanquin, even a shabby one.

Nothing. There was nothing distinctive about her to catch the emperor's eye, and not enough money on this whole street to pay the bribes that would be required to pass through the minefield that was the imperial court. The girl was doomed. And yet here she was in her richly embroidered gown, kneeling before her parents while paid women wailed.

Just as well that his presence in her palanquin would keep her from entering the competition. Once he was discovered in her conveyance, she would not be able to enter the litter. His male yang energy poisoned the virginal bower. She would have to arrange for an alternate way to reach the Forbidden City.

But there wasn't time even if her family had the money for another carriage. Not if she intended to make it to the gate by the appointed hour. Tardiness was not allowed in prospective royal consorts. Fortunately, he wasn't dooming anyone who would have made it through the Forbidden City gates. At least this way, the girl was spared the long and humiliating walk home.

All in all, he decided as he collapsed back down onto a pillow, it was better that he was here ruining her chances. And as an added bonus, he could grab another hour's sleep before he had to begin his double-damned duties in the coming Farce of Fertility.

CHEN JI YUE STRUGGLED to breathe. Excitement pounded in her blood, she was already dizzy with the noise, and yet she still could not draw a full breath. How blessed she was to be of the right age for a Festival of Fertility! Only a few hundred girls every few decades had such an opportunity! To catch the eye of the emperor was every girl's dream. That she would save her family from poverty, as well, only added to her joy. But first, she had to escape all these wailing women!

"Mama," she murmured from behind the clattering ivory beads. "Let me go. I cannot be late."

"Not yet, little heart. Show respect to your father."

She'd already bowed to her father—early this morning for real and outside again for show. "Mama, believe in me. I can do it."

Mama didn't hear her. She was busy wailing again. And worse, she would not let go of Ji Yue's hands.

"Mama…" Ji Yue began, but then her mother pulled her close.

"You won't win the emperor on beauty, Ji Yue. You must be smart. You must see what others don't and capitalize on it."

"I know. You've told me…" Ji Yue let her voice trail away. This close, she noticed there were real tears in her mother's eyes, and her heart lurched with pain. What would it be like not to see her mother's face every morning? Who would help her father with his poetry or tutor her brothers? Mama, most likely, but Mama already had plenty to do squeezing every penny so they had enough to eat.

"That playboy Sun Bo Tao was named master of the festival," her mother continued. "This is very bad and very dangerous. He is a hanger-on because of his friendship with the emperor. No title, no education, nothing but trouble. Avoid him, Ji Yue. Avoid him at all costs!"

"I know, Mama. I will stay away from him. I promise!"

"You can't! He is master of the festival! He is in charge of all the imperial virgins. Remember what I taught you—follow the Confucian virtues, think pure thoughts, but see what the men do not. I trained you to be a political wife, and the first rule of politics is to not get caught by a man of no virtue."

"I know, Mama," Ji Yue repeated. "Have faith in me. I will become the empress." If she succeeded, then her entire family would be set for generations. They would become royalty and have all the money they needed. All she had to do was catch the emperor's eye.

"Go now. Go before your father unmans himself and cries." Mama pushed her away. Ji Yue didn't need the prompting to leave. She was anxious to begin her new life even though her fingers clung to Mama's arm. But it was hard to see through her curtain of beads, harder still to walk on the high platform shoes. Thankfully, this, too, had been rehearsed.

The elder of her brothers ran to her side to escort her with all dignity to the imperial palanquin. It had been an exorbitant expense to get the conveyance, but it was the only pull her father had in the Forbidden City. He had spent a year tutoring a eunuch's nephew and in return had been promised a single favor. Papa had used it to obtain this beautiful ride to the Forbidden City. A future empress should arrive like an empress, he'd said, but that was all he could do. After this, she would have to catch the emperor's favor on her own.

The wailers grew louder as she and her brother neared the curtained palanquin. Her brother was to release her hand now and throw open the bower curtains so she could enter. He began to move away, but she suddenly gripped his arm, holding him still.

It was a silly thought, she knew, but she didn't want her brother's last sight of her to be one of extraordinary lavishness. They had so little, and even less now that so much had been spent to outfit her. She did not want her brother to see the interior luxury of the palanquin. After she became the new empress, she would send him exquisite silks as a royal gift. He need not see them now.

"Take care of Papa," she murmured as a last goodbye to her brother. "Make sure he drinks his special tea." Her brother hovered uncertainly beside her, unsure what to do now that she had changed the plan. "Go back to Papa," she said to him. "Study hard so that you can join me in the Forbidden City." There were jobs as advisors to the Dragon Throne, but only for scholars who passed the exam. She nudged him back even as she tottered forward to the bower. With one last smile that they couldn't even see, she ducked inside the palanquin.

It was dark inside, and with the beads in front of her face, she couldn't see a thing. She went by touch, crawling inside with little dignity and much speed. The cushions moved awkwardly beneath her hands until she touched a very hard one that remained stable. She pushed down, levering her weight on it.

The curtains slipped closed behind her, and one of the porters grunted as the palanquin lifted off the street. She slid off the heavy cushion onto something else. Goodness, silk was slippery. And the cushions were bizarre. The palanquin began to sway as it moved away from her family home. She wanted to peer out the curtain, but she didn't dare do something so vulgar even though the tears burned in her eyes.

She would never see her family again. Once inside the Forbidden City, no consort ever came out again. Her father might be able to arrange to visit, but such things were rare even among those more politically astute than her father. Her mother had less power, and her brothers wouldn't be allowed unless they gave up their manhood first and became eunuchs, or passed the exam and became advisors.

Ji Yue widened her eyes in the darkness, trying to dry the tears. She didn't dare cry because it would ruin the white matte that covered her face. Instead, she kicked hard at the cushions that refused to move.

"Ugh," someone grunted. Then she felt a hand grip her ankle hard.

Only years of training kept her from screaming. Ladies didn't scream. By the time she was ten, she'd faced down rats, spiders and snakes without a peep. She would not scream now when riding in an imperial palanquin. She simply kicked as hard as she could to dislodge—

"Ow! Hold still, damn it. I'm not here to rape you."

A man. Oh, heaven, a man! "Get out!" she ordered as she tried to scramble backward. She couldn't go far without falling out the back end. "Get out or I will kick you again!" It was a silly threat. He had an iron grip on her ankle.

"Quit fighting," he said in a low undertone.

"You cannot be here!" she said, and shoved as hard as she could. He lifted her leg up so that all she did was kick the air above his head. "I will scream!"

"Would you really scream? And let everyone know that a man is riding with you to the Forbidden City?"

She bit her lip, then promptly stopped since that would eat off the red paint. Her mother had told her to be smart. It was time she started using her brain instead of her extremely ineffective brawn. "What do you want?" she spat. "I have no money for you. Be thankful if you are not whipped for daring to touch an imperial consort."

He was still holding her ankle prisoner. Worse, he was putting his weight on it now as he maneuvered into a sitting position. "You're not going to be a royal bride. I'm sorry but it's true." Then he yawned while horror chilled her bones.

"You insolent pig!" She kicked again for all she was worth. He was still yawning, his head thrown back with his inhalation. Her leg slipped from his grip and caught him square in the ribs. This cut off his breath, and he doubled over with a gasp. She didn't give him time to recover but shifted and planted both feet on his hips and began to shove him right out the side of her bower.

He fought her, of course, but she was prepared. He didn't grab hold of her. Instead, his fists were filled with crumpled silk. "If I fall out now, everyone will see it," he warned. "You do not have enough ivory to silence so exciting a story—a man in a potential bride's palanquin."

She paused. One last push and he would go tumbling through the curtains out into the dirt where he belonged. "They already know from the weight," she said miserably.

"No, they don't. They carried me here, remember? They think it's just a heavy litter."

She swallowed, torn between two miserable options. Did she kick him out and pray that people believed in her purity? Never. Or did she let him stay and hope no one was the wiser. "How did you get in here in the first place?"

"I slipped in when they rested. I can slip out again at the gates. I do it all the time and no one notices."

Now that her eyes had adjusted to the dim light, she could see more of him. He was not a broad man like those carrying the palanquin, but tall like her father. His clothing was excellent, though the long queue down his back was misshapen from sleep.

"Who are you?" she asked.

"A lackey for the Son of Heaven," he said with obvious bitterness.

"Eunuch?" she asked hopefully. It was well known that some of the "cut" men were overly friendly.

He released a sharp bark of laughter at that, and she abruptly shushed him. "No," he said in a lower tone. "I am not so important as to be cut."

She frowned. "I thought all minions to the emperor were eunuchs. Who else would do the things the royals despise?"

"Me," he groused. "And a few others."

She shook her head. "I do not believe you." It was well known that except for a few intimates of the emperor, all men in the Forbidden City were eunuchs. This man couldn't be an imperial friend. Otherwise he would have his own conveyance and therefore no need to borrow hers. The eunuchs, on the other hand, would often escape into Peking for pleasure. They would also, therefore, need a secret way back into the city.

She narrowed her eyes, inspecting this man more closely. "You dress too finely to be common. You speak too well to be ignorant. And your hands…" She jutted her chin at his long, elegant fingers. "They are used to a brush and ink, not labor. You must be a secretary then, someone who works as an assistant to the emperor." She sighed in relief. "Which means you are a eunuch pretending to be whole. There is nothing exciting about an overly friendly eunuch, even if he lands in the dirt." And with that, she shoved him out of her bower.

He tumbled backward into the dust. She would forever remember the look of stunned shock on his face as he fell. And when she rolled over to peer after him, she heard the porters laugh. The Insolent One, as she now dubbed him, had landed in some rotting leaves. His fine dark clothing was smeared with grime. She couldn't see his face, though, as the porters carried her on by.

Then, with a sigh, she deftly removed two strings of ivory

beads from her headdress. She would have to bribe the porters into silence. That was a good deal of money to lose before she even reached the gates, but there was no hope for it. She couldn't risk them speaking, even about an insolent eunuch. In the end, her father's grand gesture—like all his great gifts— had cost too much money to be worthwhile.

Thankfully, she was about to change that. When she became an imperial bride, money would flow like water through her family's door. And on that happy thought, she reclined alone on the silk cushions and waited for the first test.

2

THE MASTER OF THE FESTIVAL was late. Ji Yue rolled her eyes. Of course, Sun Bo Tao, playboy of the Forbidden City, would ignore his imperial duties. He was probably in an opium daze in some woman's bedroom. But why hadn't there been provisions for that man's irresponsibility? Why couldn't they continue the inspection without him? Ji Yue tried to find out, but no one had accurate information, and she dared not risk appearing unseemly by demanding answers. Virgins were supposed to be docile and graciously accepting. So she tried to be patient as she reclined in her palanquin to wait. Dozens of girls stood around in the heat, their legs aching and their makeup running into their silks. At least she got to sit, though even she felt like she waited in an oven.

Really, the nerve of the man, making the future empress of China stay out in the heat like a drying fish! She glanced outside to see if there was any movement at all. Palanquins clogged the streets while porters squatted on their heels and threw dice. The girls were visibly wilting. One in particular drew Ji Yue's eye.

She stood nearby, her dowry in trunks around her feet. If a carriage of some sort had brought her, there was no sign of it now, and so the girl stood outside on tiny raised shoes. She looked so sad just standing there. And perhaps since Ji Yue also felt a creeping loneliness, she called out to her.

"Come, come! Sit here with me."

The girl—for she was quite young—didn't at first understand. Ji Yue had to stand up and gesture her over.

"Me, mistress?" the girl said, her eyes widening until they seemed to cover her entire face.

"Yes, yes. Why do you stand there in the heat? Where is your carriage?"

"Gone," she confessed as she waved vaguely to the west. "They said they could not wait around all day on an emperor's whim."

"Treasonous dogs!" Ji Yue spat, earning a smile from the girl. "Come, sit with me. I will say that we were carried here together."

The girl shook her head and refused to move from her trunks. "I couldn't! Not in an imperial palanquin!"

"Of course you can!" But no matter how much Ji Yue waved, the girl did not move. Finally Ji Yue went to her. "What is your name?"

"Li Fei," she answered. Then she leaned forward and confided her difficulty. "Mama says I must not sit or I will crinkle the silk."

Ji Yue smiled. "I understand. But there will be a great deal of standing to come. Wouldn't it be better to risk a few creases rather than faint when the emperor at last sees you? And besides," she added in an undertone, "your mother could not have guessed that the master of the festival would be this tardy!"

That brought a giggling nod from Li Fei. "Then I shall gratefully join you."

So began Ji Yue's first friendship within the competition. Ji Yue learned that Li Fei was from an outlying province, that she had many brothers and sisters, but that she was the only daughter of an age to apply as consort. And that she was terribly, terribly nervous about life in the Forbidden City. The next hour flew by as Ji Yue relaxed for the first time since the call went out for eligible daughters. Then a gong sounded. Loud and clear, it silenced everyone who loitered outside the gate.

"Do you think it is time?" Li Fei asked.

Ji Yue nodded, her own heart beating painfully in her throat. They both stood, but it was difficult to see, harder still to hear as a eunuch cried out orders. Fortunately, the news was whispered from servant to mistress to porter and beyond. In time, all understood that the girls were to present themselves one by one to the head eunuch, the imperial dowager consort, Kang Ci, and that playboy courtier Sun Bo Tao, master of the festival. The three would decide who was allowed to enter and who would be sent home.

"But that will take hours," Li Fei murmured. Ji Yue agreed. So they returned to the palanquin to sit longer, waiting for their inspection. Both tried to talk, but their hearts were not in it, their attention turned to the sounds that came from the front gate.

At first they heard nothing but the paid criers' announcements. "Fan Mei Lin is accepted! Fan Mei Lin enters the Forbidden City. Fan Mei Lin!"

Next came the refused, the sobbing, the wretched, even a few who had fainted dead away. No crier announced them, but whispers traveled quickly. One had been rejected for a limp, another for hair on her neck. Some had breasts too shallow to nurse a babe or ill-fated ears or feet too large. The last charge struck terror in Ji Yue's heart. Manchurian women were forbidden to bind their feet; that was a characteristic of the defeated Han people. And yet, after one hundred and fifty years of dynastic rule, the Manchu men liked tiny feet. Always the men looked to see the women's shoes.

Ji Yue looked down at her shoes. Like the curtain of ivory

beads that obscured her face, her feet were adorned with jade
and pearl drops. They were, in fact, her most expensive attire.
She and her mother had planned this, since her large feet
were her most troublesome attribute. But with feet surrounded
by jewels, any man would see wealth, not size. Just as any man
looking at her face would see ivory beads and think beauty
without judging the face beneath. Or so they hoped.

"We are next," Li Fei whispered.

Ji Yue nodded, then gripped her new friend's hand. After
a quick word to the porters to mind the luggage, the two
women walked hand in hand to the front gate.

There was a row of imperial eunuchs, dressed in finery
meant to impress. Each was designated inspector of a certain
aspect: walk, skin, teeth, ears and yes, feet. A tally eunuch
walked with each girl, adding results on an abacus. One count
for acceptable aspects. Two counts for excellence. Unfortunate aspect—one count removed. Or, worst of all, an assess-
ment of most unfortunate. Those girls were sent back to their
conveyances and told never to return.

Gold and gems disappeared quickly as bribes were slipped
from girl to eunuch. One girl just ahead of Ji Yue began with
a heavy necklace of gold links that draped almost to her knees.
By the end of the line, she wore a tiny choker of links at the
top of her gown.

But Ji Yue did not have that much bribe money. She could
not pay every eunuch for a favorable report. But she had known
that would happen; it was part of her plan. She guessed that her
father's status would gain her entry into the Forbidden City.
Except for her feet, she had no obviously ugly feature. So the
man judging feet received a pearl drop, and the tally eunuch
was given a whole string of ivory from her headdress. Beyond
that, she simply had to pray that her looks were acceptable.

She maintained hope until she entered the tent where the final tally was evaluated. Inside sat her three judges. She stepped in, making an effort to keep her steps small, her attitude reverent. But when she looked up, she saw the head eunuch, the dowager consort and the insolent eunuch from her palanquin. She stared at him, her mind working feverishly. It couldn't be possible. This couldn't be Sun Bo Tao, playboy courtier to the emperor and now master of the festival. It couldn't! And yet, as she stared at him, she knew it was.

He had changed his clothing into stunning blue silk and combed his black queue. She hadn't realized when he'd been stretched out in her palanquin how very handsome, how very tall, how very *masculine* he was! No wonder women whispered of his beauty. He had broad shoulders like a warrior, high cheekbones like a scholar, and his eyes arched in sensuous beauty as he perused her body from head to toe. Never had a man caressed her body with just a look, and she glared at him even as her breasts tightened and her knees grew weak.

He was Sun Bo Tao, the very man her mother had warned her against! And she had kicked him out of her palanquin! While she was struggling with the feelings he evoked in her, the tally eunuch lowered his head to the ground in the deepest kowtow. With shaking knees, Ji Yue performed her curtsey to the dowager consort. Then her total tally was announced with clear disdain.

"Average," the dowager consort said with a sigh. "Only average."

"Her lineage is above reproach," the head eunuch said. "Her horoscope shows four fortunate aspects."

"Yes, yes," returned the dowager consort. "I know the mother. Her father is a scholar who dreams only of the past, but he is honest, so that is something." She lifted the ivory stone that was etched with Ji Yue's name. "Very well—"

The tally eunuch beside her dropped one side of his abacas such that the beads slammed against each other with a loud clack. The head eunuch arched his brow. "Is there something to add? We are choosing the mother of the next emperor. No detail can be ignored. Speak!"

"Only what her porters say," the tally eunuch responded. "Apologies, dowager consort, but this girl is said to have consorted with a man while in her palanquin."

"That's not true!" Ji Yue cried, but no one was listening. The dowager consort had already gasped in horror and the head eunuch snatched up the ivory stone and threw it at her.

"We cannot abide a whore! How dare you insult us with your presence!"

"But it's not true!" Ji Yue cried, fury making her glare at Bo Tao. "I am not a whore!" Then she dropped to the ground to find her stone. Without that piece of ivory, she would be thrown outside in disgrace.

She saw it just before the tally eunuch planted his foot on top of it. "The porters say the man tumbled to the ground one li to the east. They laughed as he rolled into the dirt."

"That does not sound like a lover," said Bo Tao, his voice low and almost bored. "Why would he fall into the dirt?"

"Perhaps the excitement of their lovemaking—"

"It's not true!" Ji Yue repeated, her face heating until her cheeks burned. She glared up at the man responsible for her difficulties. "This is so unfair!" Then she forced herself to think rationally. She had to forget Bo Tao. He had caused her problem, and therefore was not likely to help her out of it. The tally eunuch—the man she'd just bribed to help her!—was her current enemy. She had to discredit him somehow. "You are a liar. You couldn't possibly know any of this."

"Shall I bring the porters here?" the tally eunuch asked.

Ji Yue lifted her chin. Virginal modesty be damned. She had to use her intelligence or she would be tossed out before the competition really began. "Very well," she said. "I will give you the truth. There was someone with me in the palanquin."

That silenced them all for a moment, most especially the insolent Bo Tao. He stared at her, one brow arched in surprise. Did he fear she would accuse him? Not likely. His reputation with women was well known. Any association with him would immediately label her a whore. So with a sniff of disdain, she walked to the door of the tent and pulled Li Fei inside.

"Tell them!" she ordered. "Tell them that you sat with me in the palanquin. That we spoke about your family. She is of the Tatala clan and is the daughter of Jia Hai. She likes to sing and has brothers who used to pull her hair."

The dowager consort pulled out Li Fei's carved stone. "Is this true?"

"Yes, dowager consort."

The tally eunuch stepped forward. "It is not true!" he exclaimed. "It was a man who fell from your palanquin!"

Ji Yue spun around to glare at the horrible man. "You are simply lying to get back at me," she snapped. "One of my ivory strings fell. He saw it and took it. And when I asked for it back, he refused. He knows I will accuse him of stealing, and so has created these lies to discredit me."

"Truly?" drawled Bo Tao. Ji Yue looked back at him and saw a spark of humor in the man's eyes. He was having fun? Did he think this a game? Anger built in her heart.

"Yes, truly!" she snapped. "Check his pockets. You will find my ivory beads."

The tally eunuch screamed his objection, supported by the head eunuch. Fortunately, the dowager consort agreed to the search. The tally eunuch was dragged forward by guards who had entered with Li Fei. They methodically searched his pockets, dropping gold ingots and jade bracelets onto the table. There, amid all the rich finery, sat her paltry string of ivory beads. No wonder the tally eunuch had turned on her. He likely thought she was insulting him with so wretched a bribe! But it was too late for him now with the damning evidence right before them.

The dowager consort sat back with a grunt of disgust. "Have him whipped," she muttered. The eunuch began sobbing and babbling, but no one listened as he was led away by soldiers. Meanwhile, the dowager consort poked through the pile of bribes, lifting up what she liked and gesturing to the head eunuch to take the rest. Ji Yue's lone string of ivory remained on the table. "Take it!" the dowager consort ordered. "We do not wish to be accused of thievery by the daughter of a red bannerman." She sneered the word *red* since it was the lowest level of aristocracy in China.

Ji Yue swallowed, now realizing that she had just crossed a line. All knew that the eunuchs were bribed, but Ji Yue had just exposed the reality of their corruption. A good virgin was supposed to be quiet and accepting—even of unfair practices. *Especially* of unfair practices. But what else could she have done?

With slow steps she came close enough to lift her ivory beads off the table. She replaced the string with her name stone, praying that the three judges would find it in their hearts to forgive her display of emotion. "My deepest apologies," she whispered.

Meanwhile, the cause of the problem in the first place sauntered forward. Bo Tao picked up both her stone and Li Fei's, turning to the dowager consort. "We cannot simply accept the rich ones," he drawled. "It is unfair and will sow dissension among the bannermen. They have been promised that all their daughters will have the opportunity to entice the emperor."

Ji Yue waited with breath held. Would she pass through the doors? Would she be allowed the chance to compete to become empress?

Yes! The other two grunted their acceptance. The dowager consort grabbed the two name stones and tossed them unceremoniously into a golden bowl. "Very well. But it will be on your head if they cause more disasters in the future."

Ji Yue knew better than to shout her glee, but her eyes watered with gratitude. She and Li Fei would be allowed into the Forbidden City! She kowtowed her thanks while tears streaked her white face mask. At her side, Li Fei did the same. And then more eunuchs came to escort them into the Forbidden City.

Ji Yue walked quickly, part of her afraid that the judges would change their minds if she dawdled. But even so, she couldn't resist one last glance backward. She knew Bo Tao would be watching. She'd felt the chill of his gaze on her back all through her kowtows. And now, as she met his eyes for one brief moment, she felt fear slip into her blood.

There was a price to pay for his assistance, she realized. She could see it in his eyes—that cold calculating stare that promised…something bad. And yet she felt an undercurrent of sexuality, as well. It made her breath catch and her body hum in an extremely unvirginal way. He was master of the festival and in charge of all the virgins. Did he intend to seduce her and then discredit her? That's certainly what his reputation suggested. She would have to think of a way to avoid him, to outsmart his devious plans.

But when? And how? She would be at his mercy for a week through the physical exam, the family history exam, and the artistic display. Only after those three were completed would she ever meet the emperor and have her chance to become empress. How could she avoid the master of the festival for a full week?

She didn't know, but she had to find a way. She would not let one arrogant playboy destroy her chance in this competition. She simply had to become empress. Her family's financial future depended on it.

3

Bo Tao grimaced at the noise coming from the virgins' palace. Sixty girls had passed the first examination and gained entrance into the Forbidden City. Sixty virgins covered in finery and oozing hope. Sixty women who had no idea that they would traverse a twisting maze of political intrigue just to find an outhouse. The pathway to the emperor's bedchamber would be much more dangerous.

He closed his eyes, seeing in his mind the faces of the virgins one after the other. He remembered the sobbing rejected ones and the smug wealthy ones. But bit by bit, their features all blended into one face, one girl who intrigued him as no other: Chen Ji Yue of the strong legs and fierce expression.

He'd been more amused than angry after she'd unceremoniously kicked him into the muck. Who'd have thought a little thing like her could shove the great Bo Tao into the dirt? Even the porters' mocking laughter hadn't truly soured his mood.

No, that had come later. About three minutes later when he realized he would have to walk the rest of the way to the Forbidden City. And he had to do so with muddy torn clothing, a queue that was covered with leaves and grime and a bruise on his hindquarters that ached with every step. All because the vulgar daughter of a poor bannerman decided he did not belong in her palanquin.

He knew this was not a rational anger; he had caused his own difficulties. And yet, with every step toward the Forbidden City, he plotted his revenge. True, the dowager consort and her head eunuch lackey were making most of the decisions, but only because Bo Tao didn't care which of the girls were accepted and which weren't. They were all the same, anyway. And it didn't matter to the emperor who he planted his cock in, so long as she was fertile. The dowager consort was in charge of the girls' ultimate education. So what did he—as his best friend's representative—really care about these girls? Nothing.

Nothing at all, except to see the arrogant Chen Ji Yue punished for her crime. Hours later, after he'd changed his clothing and cleaned his face, after dozens of girls had been weighed and rejected, after tedious tears or joyful squeals, she had finally shown up.

He'd seen the horror on her face when she realized who he was. She'd known she was doomed from that moment, but her pert little chin had lifted in defiance. Her assets were tallied according to her ability to bribe, her ancestry was delineated, and the dowager consort was about to give her reluctant blessing. Bo Tao's moment was at hand. He would simply step up and refuse her on some ridiculous pretext. His aching feet had been waiting all day for that very moment.

And then the tally eunuch had upstaged him. There were dozens of flaws to choose from. Her large feet or her pointy chin, for example. But the damn man had to go and pick on the one thing that was *not* her fault.

Bo Tao had almost spoken up then. Surely the man had seen her other flaws. Her tendency to speak when she ought to remain silent, for example. The way she scrabbled in the dirt for her etched stone. There were millions of reasons she was not fit to birth an emperor.

But none of them had seen what he saw. None of them knew to criticize her fierce nature. All they saw was another girl begging to be admitted to the Forbidden City. And he could not speak out against her character without revealing that he had been the one kicked into the dust.

Which meant that he had had to defend her. It had nothing to do with her excellent strategy or his surprise that a woman could think ahead enough to plan a defense. She was clearly a clever girl, and he admired her. So he'd spoken up. Because of his efforts, she was now an imperial virgin and the emperor's property. Which meant, of course, she was completely cut off from her family and friends, beset on all sides by her competitors, and he—as master of the festival—was the only path to her goal.

Did he dare toy with his best friend's property? The temptation burned in his gut. But he was beyond such childish games, he told himself. His attention was on the larger matters of state. No woman—certainly not a mouthy virgin—could tempt him away from that. His work, however unofficial, was more important. And yet, he couldn't resist thinking about her delectable lips, the saucy sway of her hips and that last look she'd given him as she walked into the Forbidden City. It was part challenge, part interest and wholly compelling.

Did he dare? Could he resist? Especially since she now owed him for his help. Bo Tao began to grin. Tomorrow's physical exam would be his next opportunity with the delectable virgin Ji Yue.

"WHY ARE YOU SO LAZY?" bellowed a male voice much too early the next morning. "An empress must be ready at all hours of the day and night!"

Ji Yue gasped and sat bolt upright in her bed. She threw

back the covers and put her feet to the floor before she realized how inappropriate that response was. Her roommate, Hua Si, of the long gold necklace that was now a choker, acted as a maiden ought; she pulled the covers up to her chin and trembled in fear at a man's presence in her room. But Ji Yue stood in her white night shift in front of...

Sun Bo Tao, the master of the festival. He stood at the doorway of their boxlike room and smirked as he stared at her bare calves and feet. Then his gaze traveled upward, and she felt the heat of his perusal slide up her legs, around her hips and then to the tips of her pointed breasts.

"How dare you enter my chamber!" she snapped as she quickly whipped the blanket off her bed and around her shoulders.

He arched his brows. "I am the master here," he drawled, somehow making his words suggestive. "I dare whatever I wish."

Ji Yue trembled even as her toes curled in delight at his dark words. She should not be intrigued by him, but he had tortured her already in her dreams. She had quivered beneath his gaze and trembled at his hold on her ankle. So his presence now seemed a simple continuation of his dreamtime seduction. But she could not allow him to distract her! So she lifted her chin and faced him eye to eye as a future empress.

"I am the emperor's concubine!" she responded tartly. "It is not seemly for you to see my sleeping attire."

"Ha!" he barked. "You are no concubine yet! And no one has privacy in the Forbidden City."

True enough. Eunuchs were everywhere. Even in the virgins' palace, they stood silent sentry over bathing, dressing, even peeing. "A virgin, however, requires modesty," she retorted. "As I am awake now, your task is done. You may go wake the others."

He arched a single black brow at her, the expression both menacing and...amused? Had she detected a glimmer of laughter beneath his dour expression? If she had, it was quickly erased.

"You will not be so impudent after today's physical examination, I wager," he said darkly. "No cosmetics. Today we will see you without lies." Then he sketched a mocking bow and withdrew from the room.

"You are so brave!" murmured Hua Si as she emerged from the blankets. "You must speak out at every turn. The emperor will be sure to notice your courage."

Ji Yue barely restrained herself from rolling her eyes at the ploy. If she continued to speak as she did, the emperor would notice her long enough to toss her outside onto a garbage heap. A woman's virtues included silence and compliance, not the acid tongue she had when that man looked at her.

She sighed and began to dress. "Do you know what is involved in the physical exam?" she asked. She had a guess, but maybe Hua Si had better information.

"I hope it involves food," Hua Si returned. "I'm starving."

Ji Yue didn't respond. She doubted she could eat. Not with the master's dire prediction poisoning the air. What did he mean? What was to happen that would make her less impudent? And what would she do without cosmetics to make herself prettier?

Without thinking, she pulled out her cream pot. The sweet scent was not makeup, per se. It was merely a special lotion to keep the skin supple and sweeten the body's smell. Was it cheating to put it on?

"What are you doing?" Hua Si gasped.

"Nothing," she lied as she stood there, cream on her fingertips.

"He said no makeup!"

"It is for the skin," she said as she dabbed a bit on her face.

"They will find out you are cheating," she said haughtily and spun out of the room, balancing perfectly on her tiny feet.

Ji Yue grimaced. Hua Si was going to tell. She quickly washed away the lotion from her cheeks but hesitated before leaving the room. There was one place where a woman's scent was strongest, one place where it most needed to be sweetened, and it was there that she'd been instructed to use the cream. Making a swift decision, she stroked a couple dabs below, resettled her clothing, then dashed out of the room.

There was no breakfast beyond the barest taste of tea. Ji Yue drank what she could, taking a moment to inspect her competition around the table. As a rule, they were all her age or younger. Though a few seemed composed, most showed their nerves in high tittering laughs or dark acerbic glares. A few had ignored the no-cosmetics rule while others displayed their natural beauty with pride.

And then *he* walked in and all other thoughts fled. She had been too flustered in the beginning to notice his attire, but now she looked closely. He was dressed in red and black court finery, but casually so. As if he wore it because he had to, not because he wished it. In that respect, he reminded her of her father. But in all other things, he was the exact opposite of her parent. Broad shoulders, commanding height and a jaw tightened in annoyance—he had a confidence that made her long to challenge him, to see if she could best him at his own game.

But then his gaze cut to hers, and her breath stopped cold in her throat. His eyes were sharp and dark, like the tip of the sharpest pin, and they pierced her straight through. Once again, she was immersed in her nighttime dream of him in her palanquin, his hand on her ankle, her knee, her thigh.

"Virgins," he said, and he seemed to sneer the word. "Virgins! You were told no cosmetics! Those who have ignored such commands will be taken out and summarily washed."

His gaze was hard on her, as if he knew what she had done. But he couldn't. Not even Hua Si knew. So she arched her own mocking brow right back. Let him find where she had placed her lotion, and then explain to the emperor how he had discovered it.

He held her gaze for a moment longer, and it was as though a lute string vibrated between them. The tone it created was too low to be heard, but she felt it deep in her womb. And the more they stared at each other, the stronger the note became.

Then a girl screamed, and he looked away. Only then did Ji Yue breathe. And once air returned to her lungs, she had the wits to look around her and see what was happening. Eunuchs were moving through the crowd of girls. They inspected faces and lifted hair to sniff at the neck beneath. Any hint of charcoal or paint and the girl was dragged away. The one who had screamed was so young—too young to be here—and the eunuch was handling her roughly. He had a bruising grip on her arm and another hand dug deep into the girl's hair as he jerked her away from the table.

Ji Yue straightened in her seat. Did they not see that the girl was terrified? Away from her family for the first time in her life, surrounded by snakes of every kind, and now manhandled by a eunuch—it was no wonder that the girl was screaming. Worse, her struggles made the eunuch more vicious as he hauled her head back and twisted her arm. And what was this girl's crime? She'd put a little red paint on her lips! That was all!

Ji Yue stood, instinctively moving to stop the eunuch's cruelty. It was a stupid move. She could not afford to bring more unpleasant attention to herself. Besides, one less girl would lessen the competition. But she feared for the girl's sanity, so she pushed forward.

"Stop that!" bellowed the master.

The sound was so commanding that everyone froze. Ji Yue was stuck in a half crouch as she maneuvered her legs and tight skirt over the bench seat. Her legs trembled as she watched the master stomp across the room to the girl, who was—thankfully—no longer screaming. But one look at her face told Ji Yue that she wasn't breathing, either. Her mouth was locked open, her eyes huge, and her skin had become paler than death.

The master stomped directly in front of the girl's view. "Breathe!" he ordered.

The girl gasped on command.

"Again!"

She did so again.

Then with a grimace, the master snapped at the eunuch. "Release her hair. What cause have you to be so cruel to these children?"

The eunuch curled his lip. "She wears paint."

"And she will be washed. But not by you." At his gesture, two new guards appeared. The master turned his attention back to the girl. At least she was breathing on her own now. "Do not fight me," he ordered, his voice low but no less powerful.

She nodded slowly.

He glanced at the eunuch. "Go wash the chamber pots, and do not show your face to me again." Then he gently took hold of the girl's arm and passed her to another eunuch, one who had kinder eyes and a softer face. "Do not disobey my orders again," he said to her.

She swallowed but was able to produce a quivering nod. Then she was led away along with nearly two dozen other girls who had applied paint of some kind. Meanwhile, Ji Yue slowly eased herself back into her seat. He saw her, of course. He seemed to be the kind of man who saw everything. As she settled back upon the hard bench, he raised his eyebrows at her.

She knew what he meant. He was asking her what exactly she had thought she could do for that girl against an army of eunuchs? She had no answer because, of course, she hadn't thought that far in advance. And what right did he have to question her, anyway, even from across the room?

So she did what her mother had taught her. She smiled sweetly with as vacant an expression as possible. If you do not wish to answer, Mama had said, then let them believe you a blank piece of art—beauty without mind—and they will forget you ever disquieted them. That was her plan and it had worked thousands of times before. Until now.

The master's lips curled in disdain. He did not hide his disgust as he turned to address the whole room. "You who remain will be taken for inspection. You will stand naked before the doctor. You will allow the physician to touch and measure and poke in whatever manner is required. You will endure this in silence, for in such a way we ensure that you are indeed a virgin."

Gasps of horror greeted these words. Most of the girls had never seen a physician before. But Mama had foreseen this particular trial and prepared Ji Yue. In fact, Ji Yue had already seen a doctor and had the process completely explained to her. Though repugnant, it would not cause her agony.

"And," continued the master with a sardonic sneer, "this examination will be repeated regularly. I suggest you guard your virginity well."

Ji Yue frowned. How could she—or any of these girls— lose their virginity here where they were surrounded at every turn? And even if there were opportunities for dalliance, who would do something so stupid?

She wasn't given time to wonder as the remaining virgins were divided into groups. Ten in each with Ji Yue as the last in her line. The first girl was taken immediately by a eunuch into a tiny room while the others sat outside and waited. And waited. And waited. An hour later, the girl reappeared, her clothing askew and muffled sobs coming from behind her curtain of black hair.

"What happened?" they all asked. "Why are you crying?"

The girl did not answer, but merely dashed away, escorted by the same eunuch who had led them here. Then it was the next girl's turn. She entered the chamber with only a soft mewl of distress, then came out wailing less than twenty minutes later.

"What happened?" she asked the eunuch.

He curled his lip in disgust. "Southern girls. Too hairy!"

"She is sent home?" asked another.

The eunuch nodded.

It took Ji Yue two breaths before she realized exactly what he meant by too much hair. Then she began to panic. How stupid had she been! Of course a check for virginity would inspect the lower body regions! Her mother had already consulted fortune tellers to learn exactly how much hair was too much or too little. Ji Yue was safe on that count. But she had put on her cream, and that certainly would be discovered!

The other girls were beginning to panic, too, and they thought about ripping out their hair before the inspection. One went so far as to try to leave. She was stopped by a pair of eunuchs guarding the exit. When she returned, tears were trembling on her lashes.

"He won't let me go back to my room."

"It won't do any good, anyway," Ji Yue inserted. "They will notice swelling if you do anything now." Just as they would notice her sweet-smelling cream.

Never mind, she consoled herself. The worst that could happen to her was that she would be bathed along with the other girls. It would be embarrassing but not fatal. Except, just then the young girl—the one who had screamed in the main room—was dragged past. Her hair was in wet clumps, her face was scrubbed raw, and her arms showed ugly welts where she had been pinched. She was sobbing again, only this time it was the miserable heartsore sobs of a woman with no hope.

Ji Yue was on her feet in a second. "Stop!" she ordered the guard. "Stop!" She went to the girl, her expression tender as she pushed the wet, stringy strands of hair out her eyes. "Surely it is not so bad as all that," she said softly.

"I am to be sent home!" the girl wailed.

Ji Yue froze, her gaze leaping to the stone-faced eunuch. "But why?"

"She was brought before the dowager consort, who declared her too ugly."

"But of course she is…is…unattractive like this! With dark bruises and raw patches."

The eunuch did not seem to care. "She was too young, anyway." And with that, he dragged her away.

Ji Yue had no choice but to sink down on her seat in fear. At her age, she did not dare appear before the dowager consort soaking wet, her hair askew, and her skin blotchy. And yet, without access to a bathing chamber, how could she wash away her cream?

No answer presented itself no matter how much she thought. And one by one, the girls disappeared into the room. Another girl was dismissed for being knock-kneed. The others came out tearful, even distraught, but they were allowed to dress for the next task: lunch with the dowager consort.

Then it was Ji Yue's turn. She stepped into the room, exhaling in relief when she saw the physician: a woman, thank heaven. She was elderly, with crabbed hands, a thin nose and a voice that sounded sharp with anger. "You're not going to cry, are you? I've had all I can stomach this morning and I'll not tolerate any more hysterics, understand?"

Ji Yue nodded, judging it wisest to keep silent.

"You're older than the other girls."

She shook her head. "No, no. I was born in the year of the rooster," she lied. "At night, too, which is an excellent time for a girl," she added, just in case the physician didn't realize that girls born during the time of "roosting" were likely to be tame and submissive.

The doctor crinkled her nose as she peered closer. "If that's true, then you will not age well."

"She was born in the year of the horse, I'd wager," a man's voice said behind her.

Ji Yue spun around, but she already knew who was there: her personal tormentor—the master of the festival. He was hidden behind the door, which was why she hadn't noticed him earlier, and he had a casual smirk on his too-handsome face. She stiffened in shock, though inside, her heart beat triple time. "Do you accuse me of lying?" she demanded.

"Of course I do," he answered calmly. "Why would you have the word 'Ji'—grain—in your name if not for being a horse?" He smiled, his expression lazy and sensuous as he listed the attributes of a girl born late in a horse year. "Which means you are destined for a hard life, Ji Yue, one of much labor. You may be broad-minded, but you lack perseverance and are incapable of keeping secrets."

"That's ridiculous!" she snapped.

He leaned forward. "If I were you, I would have lied about my age, as well."

She turned from him, unable to look him in the eye. He had named her exact reasons for lying. Though she dismissed the thought that the year and time she was born determined anything about her, she knew that others took great store by it. Especially when predicting who would make the most fertile concubine.

"Don't worry," he drawled from behind her. "Being an empress is a difficult task. I would expect her to be a woman who labors hard."

Beside her, the physician snorted through her thin nose. "All women labor hard, no matter their age. Come, come, I'm hungry. Let us see your breasts."

Ji Yue blinked, understanding hitting with a blinding flash. She was to be measured now, stripped naked and evaluated. While *he* watched.

She couldn't do it. No matter what her attributes were, he would judge her harshly, and the physician would agree. That was the way of things in China: the men made the decisions and the women had to go along with whatever idiocy resulted. If he made sure she failed the physical examination, she would be sent home within the hour! Therefore, she had to find a way to oust him from the room, and that meant appealing to the doctor.

So Ji Yue smiled sweetly and dropped into as deep a curtsey as possible. "Reverend lady," she said to the physician. "I swear I will not fight you. I will neither curse nor faint. Surely, therefore, there is no need for another here? Let the master of the festival find his lunch." That last was for him. Perhaps if he was hungry, she could induce him to leave.

"I have already eaten," he drawled. Glancing behind her, she saw that there indeed was an empty plate.

"Two steamed dumplings," the doctor groused. "But does he think to bring one to the woman who works so hard?"

"Were you hungry?" the master asked with a false smile. "My apologies. Perhaps we can speed this up." Coming forward, he pulled Ji Yue around. His touch was firm, but not bruising, and his gaze raked her body without mercy. "Can you not see what the evaluation will say?"

"That I am perfect in every way!" Ji Yue retorted.

"On the contrary," the master sneered. "Your face is barely acceptable. Eagle shaped, your nose is cursed, your tongue is worse."

Ji Yue lifted her chin. "Eagle features are striking on women. Their features command respect."

"Humph," the master retorted. "Your breasts are flat like plates. One, maybe two children at most can be nurtured before your chest is empty."

"You cannot see that!"

"Then disrobe and prove me wrong," he challenged. Before she could do more than gasp, he abruptly spun her around to stare at her bottom. "Your bottom is rounded—"

"That's good," she said as she peered over her shoulder. "It means I can be passionate. A good quality in a concubine."

"But yours is too rounded. Your passions will rule you to your detriment."

"That's not true!" she snapped as she whirled back around to face him. From behind her, the physician cackled.

"Your reaction proves his point, girl. Control yourself."

It was good advice, but Ji Yue's temper was fully engaged. "He cannot know these things!" she cried. "You must examine me to be sure."

"But why bother?" continued the master. "She is hot

tempered, so her labia will be dry, and her womb too short to support a child. The emperor will have no children by this girl."

Ji Yue clenched her hands in frustration. He was destroying her chances! Without even allowing her an examination, he was telling the doctor to report that she was unworthy of becoming the empress. "Why are you doing this to me?" she hissed at him. "Are you a cat who toys with his prey merely because he can?"

He arched a brow at her. "See?" he said to the physician. "Hot-tempered with an eagle's sharp beak for a mouth."

Turning her back on the master, she knelt before the physician. "Please, please, you must examine me. Do not let his words sway you. It is your duty to do your task as honestly as you can."

Her last words were a mistake. The physician drew herself up to her fullest height. "Do not seek to lecture me on my duties, girl. I know what I must do."

"Yes," interrupted the master with a lazy drawl, "but you need not do it on an empty stomach. Why not go now and find some excellent dumplings? Enjoy them while she meditates on the sharpness of her tongue."

The woman drew her brows together. "And then I am to return and examine her?"

The Master bowed. "Of course."

Ji Yue gasped. "But that would leave me alone with him!"

The doctor nodded. "At least you're not stupid."

Panic rose in her chest. She could not be alone with this man. He was a playboy, the emperor's intimate friend and master of the festival. No one would believe her if she said he raped her. "Please, please, Doctor. You must examine me now!"

But the doctor simply shook her head. "Won't do any good. You're all dried up right now." She glanced at the master. "Be smart, girl, and you might come out ahead." Her gaze steadied on Ji Yue. "Let him help the fertility flow. If you grow moist, my exam will be favorable."

Tears slipped down Ji Yue's cheeks. "He will rape me," she whispered.

"No," the doctor said with a surprisingly gentle voice. "No, he will not. I have known him since he was a little boy. Sun Bo Tao will threaten and tease, he will push well beyond the bounds of propriety, but he is an honorable man. Besides," she added with a glare at Bo Tao, "he knows that if he hurts you, I will see to it that the emperor finds out. No man can play with the virgins and be spared. Not even Bo Tao, who has no status here except for the emperor's whim."

Ji Yue looked up, feeling hope and despair clash in her heart. As much as she might pray that Bo Tao was honorable—was simply just teasing her for some sick reason of his own—she did not believe she was that lucky. Or that any man could really be so honorable. So she grabbed the woman's hands and begged, "Please, don't go."

"She has no choice," Bo Tao said, his voice cold. "I am the master of the festival. She cannot disobey me." Then he stepped around and opened the door. "Go and eat something, Doctor."

The woman slowly disentangled herself from Ji Yue. "I eat very quickly," she said. Then with a last apologetic shrug, she left. The master followed a step behind, firmly shutting the door behind her.

Ji Yue was alone with her nemesis.

4

JI YUE SCANNED THE ROOM for a way to escape. He blocked the door, and there was nowhere else to run. "Why are you doing this?" she demanded. She didn't think he would answer. She asked only because she was stalling as she figured out a strategy. But to her surprise, he seemed to think deeply about her question.

"I don't know," he finally said. "You are different."

She looked away. She knew she was different. And in China, different was very bad. "I'm smart," she countered. "And strong. I will make a good empress."

He touched her cheek, lifting her pointy chin with a firm stroke. "I begin to think you are right. Yi Zhen could do worse than marry you." Then he smiled. "Don't be afraid; I will not hurt you."

"Of course you will!" she shot back. "Why else would you maneuver me this way? Why else would we be alone together!"

"I did not hurt you in the palanquin," he said.

"You did not have time! I kicked you out."

He grimaced. "Yes, I know. My ribs still hurt."

She stared at him in confusion. He blocked the door, but he made no move to rape her. Up until now, he had merely been a man who mentally tortured her, a man who blocked her path to the emperor's bed. But for the first time, she actually looked closely at his face. She expected that his features would be soft and lax with the indolence of a courtier, but what she saw instead was a hardened jaw and clear eyes in an unsmiling face. This man might be many things, but he was not soft. And that thought surprised her almost as much as it excited her. "What do you want of me?" she asked.

He smiled, and this time there was no mockery in his expression. "To test you, Chen Ji Yue. To find out what kind of woman you are. Do you wish to become empress?"

She nodded. "You know I do."

"Then what will you do? As the doctor said, you will not pass this test today. You are hot-tempered. Your fertility is already dried up."

"You don't know that!"

He stepped forward. "I do. But if you like, you can check for yourself. Think of the place between your thighs. Is it wet and supple?"

Ji Yue gasped, her thoughts going straight to that part of her body. And then she remembered what she had done to keep her private area sweet and supple. She swallowed, trying to act casual, but fear ate at her reason. "Why…why would you ask about that place?"

His eyes narrowed. She wanted to look away, but she could not when he stared at her so intently. "You have done something," he said. "Something that no one else knows about." His brows drew together in anger. "Chen Ji Yue! Are you a virgin?"

"Of course!" she cried. "Of course I am! I have done nothing but—" She swallowed, cursing her errant tongue. What was it about this man that made her stupid with her words?

"But what?" he demanded.

"It is nothing," she whispered. "Just a cream to keep the skin moist and the petals blossoming."

His eyebrows shot up. "And did you apply this cream today?" he asked. "Despite my express warning against wearing cosmetics?"

"It is not a cosmetic! It is fruit and herbs. It's not a paint at all. More like food for…for women." She looked at him in misery. Her face burned with shame. "Please help me," she whispered. "The doctor is sure to notice."

"My, my," he drawled. "You do have a problem." He did not sound angry, merely pensive. She did not dare hope that he would help her for no compensation, but she was desperate.

"Bring me a bucket with water. I…I have jewelry. I can pay."

He reared back in anger. "Do not seek to bribe me, girl!"

"Then what do you want?"

He smiled slowly, but his eyes remained grave. "I cannot bring you water. It would be noticed and even I cannot break the rules."

She took a step forward. "You are breaking the rules now by being alone with me. Say that someone grew ill, that you wish to clean up the mess."

"I would send a eunuch for that."

She grimaced, her ideas—and her time—running out. "What is the punishment for wearing cosmetics?"

He sighed. "You have already seen the punishment. The eunuchs are not kind when they bathe you. And they will be especially cruel where you are most dirty."

She winced. "Why do you allow such men here?"

He folded his arms. "I do not allow anything. In fact, I have counseled Yi Zhen against it, but we always meet with the same answer."

"What is that?"

"That eunuchs have been a way of life in the Forbidden City long before the Manchu came and will continue long after we are gone."

She looked away, cursing herself for her vanity this morning and wondering if she had thrown away her chances with that one simple act. "I meant no harm. It is just a sweetening cream." Then she swallowed and forced herself to beg. "Help me please. What should I do?"

He waited while she twisted her fingers together in anxiety. His look was pensive, but his eyes seemed to burn. "There is a way, you know, to drown out the scent of your…your fruit and herbs. A way that the doctor will never notice and will boost your attractiveness as an imperial consort."

She bit her lower lip, barely daring to hope. Could he truly wish to help her? Of course not, and yet what choice did she have? "More creams?" she asked.

He smiled, and she was momentarily struck silent by the beauty in his face. Normally he scowled at the women who plagued him, but for this moment he looked different. Not gentle so much as less fierce. More…seductive. And again she was startled by how appealing that made him.

"I will not surrender my virginity!" she stated fiercely. "I will fight you if you try!"

"Of that I have no doubt," he said dryly. "No, I refer to the stages before surrender."

She frowned, extraordinarily suspicious but also a little intrigued. Though her mother had explained lust in great detail, most especially what it could drive a man to do, she had never spoken about the steps of love or of the act itself. "What stages?"

"You wish to know?" he asked.

"I wish to become an empress," she snapped.

"Then allow me to touch you and your fertility will never be in question."

"No touching!" she cried as she backed away.

"I cannot do it any other way," he responded. "You need only unbutton your blouse. I will touch your breasts."

She shook her head, her heart beating so loud it seemed to echo in her mind.

"You will show me your breasts, anyway, as part of the examination."

"But I will lose my virginity!"

He stared hard at her. "Do you truly not know how it is done?"

She flushed so hot her ears burned. "I have seen dogs. I...I know the essence, but a touch one place will lead to more. And you are stronger than I."

"Then take this." He handed her his empty plate. "If I touch more than you wish, then you may break it on my head. Do it hard enough and I will not be touching anything again for a very long time."

She hesitated a moment, then grabbed the plate from him. Whatever she decided, she would feel better with a weapon in her hand.

"Decide quickly. The doctor will be back soon."

That brought a return of her fears and a swift decision. With a deep breath, she began unbuttoning the clasps at her neck and then down along her side. All too soon, her blouse was pushed away, the silk dropping uselessly to the floor. Below it, her diamond-shaped undergarment of soft cotton was already stained from perspiration. The ties pulled at her neck and back, but her entire front remained covered by the too-thin fabric.

"Take it all off," he said, his voice low and thick.

She lifted her chin and stared at him. She had to do this, she reminded herself. And truthfully, a kind of madness had gripped her. She wanted to do this. She wanted to see his face when her flesh was bared to his eyes. So while one hand still gripped the plate, the other resolutely untied her undergarment. And inside her, the blood seemed to beat faster, wilder, with a daring she found as exciting as the man who stood before her.

"Not flat plates, after all," he murmured. His face was no longer pinched, but his eyes still held that intensity she both feared and enjoyed. "Your breasts are bells arching outward." He spoke as if to himself while one hand lifted to touch her. "They say that women with bells mature young and have very high desires." His hand stopped, and his gaze leaped to hers. "I am going to touch you now. Do not be afraid."

She wasn't. Looking in his eyes, she didn't see anger or vengeance. She wondered for a moment if this was the look of lust, but he did not have the signs that her mother had told her of. His eyes did not pinch nor did his mouth pull back like a dog in heat. If anything, he had the look of reverence.

"Your skin is flawless," he said. "It would glow in candlelight."

He touched her. With his long elegant fingers, he stroked the side of one breast and fire trailed in his wake. She gasped at the feel, and he smiled. Then he curved his hand around the outside before brushing his thumb across her peaked nipple.

She trembled. It started in her belly, but it traveled outward, making her breath stutter and her heart race. He moved closer, his hand still caressing her breast.

"What...what are you doing?" she gasped, though the answer was perfectly obvious.

"You are safe. Keep the plate handy."

She had forgotten it. With shaking hands, she gripped the fine porcelain tight, but she didn't do anything with it. He moved around behind her, his one hand still stroking. Her breast felt hot and large in his hand, and her back tingled with awareness of him. And then, every so often, he would pinch the nipple and she would shudder at the flash of sensation that burst through her thoughts. Her whole body now beat with a wildness and a hunger she'd never felt before.

His free hand slipped around her rib cage to lift her other breast. He leaned against her back, pressing her forward so that her legs pushed against the physician's table. She was pinned between him and the table while his breath brushed hot across her cheek. She felt surrounded by him, completely and totally within his power.

"Do you know what leads to fertility?" he whispered into her ear.

She shook her head. It was hard to think with his hands rolling over her breasts.

"Passion, Chen Ji Yue. A passionate woman is a fertile woman." He pinched her nipples—both at once—and she cried out in her surprise. "What you feel right now is passion, and it is what all these physicians, eunuchs and courtiers are looking for."

"What of the emperor?" she gasped. "Does he look for this as well?"

"Him most of all," he said into her neck. Then she felt his tongue, hot and wet as he stroked the skin behind her ear.

"Oh!" she gasped.

"Lean forward," he murmured.

She did because she liked what he was doing. The feel of his tongue overwhelmed her senses, and his hands had not stopped moving in mesmerizing caresses all over her breasts.

"You smell sweet, Ji Yue. I think your cream has grown stronger."

She tensed. "But it can't! You said—"

"Let me see if I can wipe some away."

He pressed her forward even farther and one of his hands abandoned her breast to slip down to her knee. With quick movements, he pulled her skirt up to her waist.

"No…" she murmured, but he must not have heard her.

"Widen your legs for me, Ji Yue," he said. "I must have access to wipe the cream away."

She did not intend to move, but her legs were so weak. He pinched her nipple again, and as she arched in reaction, his leg slipped between hers. And then his hand was where no man's hand had ever been.

"There is so much cream here!" he said as he began to stroke her.

Oh, the feeling was amazing. She could barely breathe for the wonder of it. It was as if he coaxed a flame hotter and brighter with every touch. The flame burned through her belly, sending sensation up her spine. Then he widened his hand and burrowed deep with his fingers while she…she…

She whipped around and slammed the plate against his head. It took all her strength and she collapsed sideways after the impact. But that gave her the space she needed to shove him away. "You said you would only touch my breasts!" she accused.

He had fallen a step backward, but he was still standing. She hadn't hit him hard enough, she supposed, and now she had a new problem. What would he do to explain the welt he sported on his temple?

"You told me I could hit you," she said, struggling to put force into her voice. But she didn't have the breath, and her heart was beating so fast! "You told me to do that if you touched me somewhere else."

He lifted his head and she saw that she had cut him, too. Blood dripped down the side of his head and his eyes blazed with fury.

"You told me I should hit you!" she cried again. She had

already pulled down her skirt, and now she tried to retie her undergarment one-handed. Her other hand gripped the largest shard of plate that she could reach. "You told me—"

"So I did," he said. He rubbed his hand over his temple then grimaced when his palm came away glistening with blood. "Cover up. The doctor will be here soon."

With shaking hands, she retied the cotton underdress, then pulled on the silk blouse, fastening the clasps with one hand. Just as she finished the last button, the door burst open and in walked the physician.

The woman froze on the doorstep, and her eyes narrowed on the tableau before her: Ji Yue flushed and breathing hard; the master with blood smeared down his cheek. And of course, the plate pieces shattered about the room. It wouldn't be hard to guess what had happened. The question was: would she blame the master? Or Ji Yue?

With a snort of disgust, the doctor threw a towel at him. "You're disgraceful," she snapped. She turned to Ji Yue. "Put the plate down. You're safe now."

Ji Yue slowly released the plate shard. She had to consciously will her hand to open. When the porcelain clattered to the floor—shattering anew—the woman huffed in disgust. She went to the door and called in a eunuch to clean up the mess.

"Clumsy girl has broken a plate," she groused to the eunuch. Then she looked hard at Ji Yue. "Fortunately, the emperor has many plates. You might be wise to keep an extra handy for whenever you break one again."

"Always," she answered softly, her gaze going to the master. "I won't be caught without one again."

"You weren't caught without one now," he returned, but she detected a note of humor in his complaint.

The plate pieces were swept up, the eunuch sent away, and

then the doctor shut the door. She turned to the master. "You should see the emperor's physician for that cut."

He pulled the towel away from his head. "It was only a scratch."

The woman snorted. "You are staying, then."

The master smiled. "It is my sworn duty to the emperor as master of the Festival of Fertility."

"Humph," she retorted. Then she turned back to Ji Yue. "All right then, girl, let's see what damage he's done."

Ji Yue had been standing mutely to the side, doing her best to stop trembling. Soon, very soon, she would be able to disappear into her room and think on what had happened. But at the doctor's words, she started in surprise.

"What?"

"Your examination, girl. Don't tell me he has stolen your wits."

"My, um, I mean…no. I have my wits."

"Then undress. Let me see what has so intrigued Sun Bo Tao."

Ji Yue stared at the physician, her misery now complete. After everything she'd just endured, she still had to go through the physical examination. And in front of the master! But what choice did she have? None. So she submitted. Button by button, she undid what she had just fastened. And as she worked, she plotted her revenge.

5

SHE HAD HIT HIM with a plate. Even as he felt the throbbing of his temple, Bo Tao could still not believe she had hit him. No woman had ever dared do that to him, and he didn't know whether to be angry or impressed. He settled for being intrigued.

He leaned against the wall, his thoughts still whirling, and prepared to watch a most interesting examination. An honorable man would leave, since he had already compromised Ji Yue enough. But he could not seem to leave her alone; she'd dominated his thoughts since she'd shoved him out of her palanquin yesterday. Was he intrigued by her audacity? Fascinated by her intelligence? Or just lustful for her sweet curves? Yes to all. Which meant that even when his intention to simply talk to her alone, he wound up with his hands on her breasts and her legs spread beneath him. She made him lose control, and that was both dangerous and wildly exciting.

He folded his arms across his chest and watched while the virgin glared daggers at him. No hysterics, no whimpering, just darkly plotted revenge. He was rather excited to imagine what she could do to hurt him. But mostly he was aroused simply smelling her scent in the air and seeing her glorious breasts once again revealed to his gaze.

"Not flat, then," said the physician as she made notes on her paper. "Good breadth of lungs and a fine skin color, if somewhat flushed." She flashed Bo Tao a harsh look. He smiled in response. Women's physician Xie Yan had been his mother's doctor and had known him since birth. She would tolerate his excesses so long as no lasting harm was done. And besides, as master of the festival, he had the right to supervise any examination, even one this intimate.

"Very well," Xie Yan snapped, her glare still trained on him though she spoke to Ji Yue. "Remove the rest."

Bo Tao's mouth was dry. Finally he would see what he had touched. In the heat of a Peking summer, no woman wore underthings below her hips, and certainly not a virgin intent on seducing an emperor. And so he watched, his cock painfully hard, as button by button her sweet bottom was revealed.

"Excellent shape," Xie Yan said.

He couldn't agree more. Her bottom was rounded and lifted. Perfect. Ji Yue stepped out of the skirt to stand naked, her back to him. He admired the sensuous sweep of her spine, the rounded curve of her behind, and the long, firm shape of her legs.

"Mole on upper left thigh."

Ji Yue twisted toward the doctor. "Is that bad?"

"No, no. Simply a mark. It might denote something significant to the fortune tellers, but I don't know what. I just have to write it down."

He wanted to kiss that mole. He wanted to roll his tongue over it and feel the shift in texture. And he wanted to let his lips travel across her thigh and up to taste her sweet cream.

"Now stand still. I need to take some measurements."

Xie Yan brought out her tape and began to measure, beginning with Ji Yue's head. Nothing was neglected from the length of her nose, the width of each breast, and the size of her hips. Ji Yue endured it all, her anger still a palpable force in the room. Her only hesitation came as her feet were measured. She flushed a dark red as the size was announced.

Interesting, Bo Tao thought. He could see nothing but natural, beautiful feet with well shaped toes and a high arch.

"On the table, if you please," instructed the physician.

Ji Yue shifted to climb up, and he knew he'd soon see all. What he focused on instead was the way her hands shook. She was not as sanguine as she appeared, and who could blame her? In a small deference to her feelings, he did not move to a better viewing position. He doubted he could walk smoothly anyway. So he remained at the top of the table, just past her left shoulder. As she lay down, he saw the slow reveal of her body before him. The length of her legs, and the rounding of her hips. He gloried in the rise and fall of her breasts, the sensuous indent at her belly, and the broad width of her womb. She would be able to carry babies well.

The doctor placed herself at Ji Yue's feet. "You must understand that I have to measure everything, do you not?"

Ji Yue nodded. Were there tears in her eyes? Bo Tao frowned. Certainly most of the girls sobbed at this point, but Ji Yue had been so stonelike throughout the examination. It startled him that she showed feeling now. But of course she would. No virgin suffered this examination calmly. Still, the sight of her moist lashes unsettled him.

"You must bend your knees and slide down the table," Xie Yan instructed.

Ji Yue took a stuttering breath. Her gaze was fixed firmly on the ceiling as she used her hands to scoot herself lower on the table. Bo Tao watched in growing confusion as she lifted her knees but kept them pressed tightly together. He did not understand his reaction. He was waiting for just this moment; for the sight of her spread thighs, her woman's hair open and glistening in the light. But this did not feel like a glorious moment. What was wrong with him? He had seen scores off sobbing virgins—on this day alone. And yet this woman's tears disturbed him.

The doctor put her hands on Ji Yue's knees. "You must open for the measurements," she said. "It is a requirement for every empress." Then she pressed firmly down and gradually spread Ji Yue's legs. The movement was stuttering, the resistance obvious, and a single tear slipped down the side of her face.

Something broke inside Bo Tao. "Enough!" he bellowed, stepping forward. He grabbed Ji Yue's clothing as he moved and quickly pushed it at her. "No more examination today."

The doctor looked up, her eyes hard. "You know this must be done. Are you afraid to see the consequences of your own debauchery?"

"I have done nothing!" he snapped. "You can see that she is moist and supple. There is good color and size." He did not know that for sure, but it didn't matter. If he said it, it would be so recorded.

"And her virginity?"

He swallowed. Even he could not forge that. If a false woman passed through to meet the emperor, it would be his head.

"Very well—check it quickly." he snapped, his anger not at the doctor, but at himself. Why did *this* virgin's tears upset him so? He glanced down at Ji Yue, emotion churning in his gut. "Be gentle!" he ordered.

"Now he worries about gentleness!" the physician muttered. Then her attention shifted to Ji Yue. "I have to touch you very intimately. I will go slowly, and it should not hurt. Are you ready?"

Ji Yue nodded, then firmly shut her eyes. Bo Tao knew the

exact moment the doctor touched her intimate folds. Ji Yue jerked, gasping in surprise.

"You are doing very well," the doctor said.

Ji Yue released a soft murmur of distress. Unable to stay apart from her, Bo Tao moved quickly to the top of the table. He pressed his hands to her shoulders. "It is nearly done," he said. He had hoped that she would open her eyes and see that he was looking at her face, not her groin. But she kept her eyes shut tight.

Then, finally, the doctor straightened and stepped away. "Virginity intact."

Bo Tao barely heard the words. His attention was centered on Ji Yue as she rolled onto her side. There were no blankets in the room, but her clothing was there. He used it to gently cover her most private area.

"You have done your duty, physician Xie Yan," he said. "You may go now."

The doctor looked up from her notations. "You wish to be alone with her?" Shock colored her tone.

"She has nothing to fear from me," he growled. "She never did."

Silence reigned for a moment, and then he heard the doctor's "Humph." He had won. She would leave and say nothing about it to anyone. Meanwhile, he knelt down beside the table. Ji Yue's face was very pale, and her eyes were still shut tight. He brushed a lock of hair behind her cheek. "Her report will read excellence in every way," he instructed.

"Of course," the doctor answered. "She *is* excellent in every way. And with her fire, she will make a fine empress."

Bo Tao jolted at the thought. He had forgotten that she was destined to be Yi Zhen's wife. The emperor could not fail to see how perfect she was. And while that thought soured in his gut, the physician collected her things and left.

"She is gone now. You are safe."

Ji Yue opened her eyes, fixing him with a hard stare. She didn't speak, but Bo Tao didn't care. Her eyes told him that she was recovering. Her voice would return soon enough.

"I am sorry you had to endure that." He swallowed. He was on the verge of promising that she would never have to undergo the ordeal again, but that would be a lie. All brides would be rechecked before the wedding. Up until the final selection, virginity must be assured. So he held back his promise even as he tried to help her in other ways. "You can get dressed now, if you like. Are you hungry? I can send for some food."

She still didn't speak, and her glare hadn't softened, but she did shake her head as she pushed up from the table. He cupped her elbow, helping her to rise, but she shrugged him off. Realizing she didn't want him to touch her, he stepped back, though he felt the separation keenly.

She kept her skirt lying over her private area as she quickly tied on her undershift. He mourned the covering of her beautiful breasts, but he didn't say a word. She pulled on her blouse next, buttoning it with deft moments. Then she paused, lifting her head to fix him with a dark glare.

She needed to stand to pull on her skirt, but that would expose her again. Though it gave him a physical pain, he nodded his understanding and turned around. He would not watch her woman's glory glisten as she dressed. But oh, how his loins ached. He was undressing her again in his imagination when she finally spoke.

"Do I go now to luncheon with the dowager consort?" Her voice was thick and low, but there was strength in her tone. She would not be deterred from her task.

He shook his head as he turned around. "It has already begun, and it would not be wise to show up late."

Her lips compressed in a tight frown.

"It is better if you don't appear. She is looking for girls to reject. If she does not see you, she cannot dismiss you."

Ji Yue nodded, but still didn't look at him. Given how direct her stare had been earlier, this sudden uneasiness bothered him. "Why are you nervous?" he asked.

At that she lifted her chin and met his gaze. He could tell she had to force herself, and he trembled inside at the anxiety he saw in her eyes. "What do you want of me?" she asked. "Why have you singled me out?"

He had no answer for her. In truth, he had been wondering the same thing. Before he'd met her, the idea of seducing a virgin—much less a potential imperial concubine—held no appeal whatsoever. But this was different. Chen Ji Yue was very different indeed.

Without a way to answer her, he dodged the question. "Many girls have asked for baths after their examination," he said. "I can take you to the bathing chambers now so that you can wash in private. I must see to the removal of the girls dismissed at lunch. You will have as much privacy as can be found in the Forbidden City."

She nodded her acceptance. "That would be fine."

So he escorted her to the bathing area. He ordered fine linens for her use and special foods for her lunch. And then in an act of supreme self-sacrifice, he left her alone. For now….

6

JI YUE FELT LIKE DANCING! She had passed the physical exam with excellent marks, and now she was going to meet the emperor!

This was not the usual course of events. Normally, no virgin would see the emperor until the final selection day, but something marvelous had happened. The vicious Taiping rebels had been defeated and one of their leaders was dead! The emperor had declared everyone in the Forbidden City would feast in celebration. There was to be a banquet, and he would be there!

Ji Yue decided that she would do whatever it took to shine before the emperor. Unfortunately, all fifty of the remaining virgins had the exact same thought as they dressed for this important event.

Hair always took the bulk of time as it was wrapped around boards then glued into place. Jewels made to look like butterflies or flowers were intertwined with the strands and cemented in. Finally, heavy white paint would be stroked onto each girl's skin and accented with delicate red or black. An empress would have no less than five servants to assist her. The virgins, on the other hand, were given one eunuch per five girls. Though they had the whole day to prepare, no servant could possibly fill the demands of so many girls intent upon impressing an emperor.

The first arguments began in the bathing chamber around noon. One girl claimed another had passed gas and should be removed from the festivity for fouling the water. By two, someone accused another of stealing her cosmetics. The argument became so heated that Bo Tao was summoned. Upon searching the accused trunks, he found dozens of stolen items. The thief was immediately expelled, but such swift action only increased the problem.

Suddenly everyone knew of a thief or a liar who should also be tossed out of the Forbidden City. That occupied him for another two hours until he declared that one girl's accusations were completely fabricated. Ji Yue could have told him that at the beginning, but he was a man and felt he had to investigate. In the end, he came to the correct conclusion and expelled the accuser.

In truth, Ji Yue was impressed by his methodical investigation. He remained unswayed by tantrums or hysterics. Seeing that there were risks to groundless accusations, the virgins then turned their rancor on the hapless eunuchs. Even with the aid of the head eunuch, Bo Tao could not stem the tide of women who absolutely demanded satisfaction for one slight or another.

By the time Ji Yue's roommate began screaming, poor Bo Tao looked stooped with exhaustion. His clothing was stained from thrown cosmetics, his queue was distorted and his eyes blazed with fury. The man had reached his limits.

Unfortunately, Hua Si did not seem to realize her danger. Bo Tao stood in the doorway, his mouth tightening into a hard flat line while Hua Si screeched as if a monkey had bitten her rear. Ji Yue tried to shrink as far away as possible, which in their tiny boxlike room wasn't far at all. And then Bo Tao spoke, his tone harsh and cold.

"Your noise is offensive!" he bellowed. "Explain yourself!"

Hua Si blinked. Surely, thought Ji Yue, the girl would see her danger and moderate her tantrum. Apparently not, because the spoiled beauty actually stomped her foot in irritation.

"Someone spit in my paints!" she wailed.

Ji Yue rolled her eyes, not even bothering to look at the cosmetics. It could be a serious problem if the heavy white paint was too thin. The color would be blotchy when applied and wear off in streaks throughout the evening. But someone would have to spit a lot for such a problem to occur. Hua Si didn't seem to care, though, as she folded her arms, peered down her nose, and demanded new paints.

"No," answered Bo Tao.

Hua Si was stunned. "No? No!"

He smiled. "No." Then he turned and began walking down the hallway.

Hua Si stormed after him. "Don't you want to know who committed this crime? Don't you need to investigate?"

Bo Tao turned and looked not at Hua Si but at Ji Yue. There was a question in his eyes that she didn't understand. Did he think she had spat in the girl's cosmetics? Ji Yue felt her mouth open in shock and she straightened to defend herself. But Bo Tao simply shook his head and turned his attention back to Hua Si.

"Virgin Gao Hua Si, I don't care if someone pissed in your pot. Finish your dressing and be done with it!"

Hua Si gasped, the shock of his vulgar words upsetting her delicate constitution. She began to shake. "But what am I to do?" she wailed.

"I suggest you eat your poisoned makeup. Perhaps that will silence you."

Ji Yue winced at his ridiculous suggestion. Such a comment would send her roommate into a tirade that would last for hours. Bo Tao would be gone, of course. He looked like he was about to bolt, anyway. But Ji Yue would have to endure hours of the spoiled beauty's hysterics. So she pushed up from her table, acutely aware that her hair was undone, falling about her face in an unruly mass. But she'd never get the eunuch's help if Hua Si was throwing a fit.

"Eating is an excellent suggestion, Master Sun Bo Tao," she said. "Soothing tea and a small dumpling would be a great substitute for the paints. In the meantime, Hua Si, you may use my cosmetics."

"What use would I have for your pig slop?" Hua Si screeched. The sound was loud enough that Bo Tao winced.

"I have heard, master," Ji Yue continued, "that a lack of food sometimes makes women unsettled. It is our delicate constitutions, you know. And we have had nothing since morning tea. Do you not recall how excited we all were when we heard of tonight's celebration? Many of us were too excited then to eat a bite."

Bo Tao narrowed his eyes at her in confusion. "They are hungry?" he gasped.

"Perhaps you are hungry, you ugly cow," roared Hua Si, but she did not get to rant for long as the head eunuch came bustling in from another room.

"Who is hungry? What ridiculous nonsense! Do you think we have food to spare, girl? For testy spoiled virgins who beat their servants and screech like fishwives?"

Ji Yue bowed slightly in a show of shame. "My apologies, head eunuch. I merely thought that with mouths full, the virgins would have no breath to complain."

"Truer words could not be spoken," said Bo Tao. "Head eunuch, can we not bring some sweet dumplings? Surely the kitchen will have made enough to spare."

The cut man bristled with indignation. "And who will fetch and serve this bounty? You? Her? My eunuchs are too busy for such nonsense."

Hua Si sneered. "I have told her she eats too much, but she is from the country and does not understand that life in the Forbidden City requires sacrifice."

Ji Yue ground her teeth. "I am not from the country," she said as calmly as possible.

"You see?" Hua Si put in with a roll of her eyes. "She argues about everything. So demanding." Then she turned around and went to the mirror. With a huff of disgust, she began to apply her "poisoned" paint to her face.

Meanwhile, the head eunuch sniffed disdainfully at Ji Yue. "I do not like girls who constantly complain, Chen Ji Yue." With that he spun away.

Ji Yue stared at his retreating back, the unfairness of it all making her eyes tear. Though the emperor chose his brides, the head eunuch controlled a concubine's life. He supervised servants and housing. He managed resources between the harems. And most important, he was the one who brought brides to the emperor's bed. She could not become pregnant with the next emperor if she never graced the man's bed. And she would never grace the imperial bedchamber if she made an enemy of the head eunuch.

Meanwhile, in a nearby room, another argument erupted and something fragile was smashed. In her mirror she saw Bo Tao wince at the noise.

"Can you dress your hair yourself?" he asked.

She blinked. Had he been speaking to her? "Master?"

"Your hair? Can you do it by yourself?"

She glared at him. What a ridiculous question! No woman could create the elaborate hair displays alone. But she was not in a position to argue, so she gave the answer he wanted. "I will do my humble best."

"Good," he said. Then he snapped his fingers at the eunuch assigned to help them. "You! Come with me to the kitchens." With that he left, taking her only help with him.

Trays of tea and dumplings arrived a half hour later. No one thanked her for the idea, not that she expected anyone would. But she didn't even get any of the food since she was busy struggling with her hair. Someone had to hold the board in place while the hair was wrapped and glued. Thankfully, Li Fei was able to help. Though there had been little time to further her friendship with the girl from the carriage, Li Fei was naturally kind, had quick fingers and an easy smile. Together, they dabbed glue as quickly as possible, secured the board, but only partially set the butterfly hairpin. Then they ran together to dinner.

They slipped inside with the last of the virgins, grateful that there was adequate seating. Otherwise, their tardiness would have them eating outside with the disgraced eunuchs. Flashing a grin of excitement to her friend, Ji Yue settled down at the table and tried to look like an empress. Unfortunately, among all the fine silks and beautiful girls, she very much feared that she looked more like Hua Si's impoverished cousin.

The emperor sat at a table on the opposite side of the room. From this distance, all Ji Yue could see was his exquisitely embroidered clothing and his dark black hair. Still, she felt a tingle of excitement race down her spine. She had never been this close to the emperor before, and the feeling made her belly jump and her voice high. The other virgins were equally excited, equally delighted. But of course there was no hope of attracting his attention from across the room. So after repeatedly craning her neck to look in his direction, Ji Yue settled in to enjoy her meal.

It was between the tenth and the eleventh course that the emperor stood up. The reaction at the virgins' tables was immediate. Chopsticks clattered to the table, and hair was quickly patted into place. Ji Yue was not immune to the need to primp as her butterfly pin had once again dropped down behind her ear where no one would see it.

The emperor left the festival hall. All the virgins—Ji Yue included—returned to their food with a dispirited frown. Ji Yue's stomach was full, but she didn't know when she'd be able to eat again. She would take what she could now with no worry that the emperor would catch her with her mouth full. A door opened and closed behind her, but she paid no attention. Eunuchs went in and out that way all the time.

"Which is the virgin who dared hit you with a plate?"

Stunned gasps surrounded her at the man's voice. Ji Yue gasped as well, but she was eating. The result was a very unempresslike gurgle and a very undemure choking sound.

"It was an accident, Yi Zhen."

Ji Yue felt her blood run cold. She knew that voice. It was Master Sun Bo Tao, and he was speaking the childhood name of the emperor. Which meant both the master and the emperor were right behind her!

"On your temple?" the emperor responded. "Was she throwing plates around to hit you so high? Ha! Or were you on your knees before her?"

Ji Yue barely heard the question over the roaring in her ears. She needed to cough the food out of her windpipe, yet to do such a thing before the emperor would be ghastly. But she had to breathe! She began to cough.

"So, Bo Tao, which one is she?"

"The one so frightened by your presence that she cannot breathe."

She heard footsteps behind her and hastily tried to regain some composure. At least her coughing had subsided and she could breathe. There was a touch on her shoulder, and she was forced to turn around. It was the emperor, of course, looking down at her from a vast height. She was aware that her spasms had dislodged her hair. She could feel it slipping away from the board and hiding her jade butterfly pin. She gazed up at the emperor with miserably hopeful eyes. Would he see past her disheveled appearance to the woman beneath? Of course not. For all that he was the emperor, he was also a man. He saw nothing but the superficial.

She had to do something exceptional very soon. Her mother's words rang through her thoughts. *You cannot be beautiful, so be smart.* The other girls were bowing to the emperor, murmuring their names along with their greetings. When it was her turn, Ji Yue did the same, her voice husky and thick from her coughing.

"Humph," the emperor said. "You do not look so bold now. Tell me, Chen Ji Yue, why did you hit my friend with a plate?"

Ji Yue glanced at Bo Tao, her mind filled with the memory of his hands on her breasts, of her heart beating so fast as he slid his fingers ever lower. She felt her face heat beneath her white paint and saw an answering panic in his eyes. Did she tell the truth? Did she say that the emperor's best friend had done things to her that no virgin allowed? And that part of her still moistened at the thought of him doing them again?

She swallowed and ducked her head. "It was an accident, great emperor," she said. "I…tripped and the plate flew from my hand. I was merely clumsy."

"Humph. I suppose that could be true." He flashed Bo Tao a look filled with humor. "But I doubt it." Then he snorted as he scanned the sea of hopeful virgin faces. "A girl's virtue is always in danger even in the Forbidden City. Your clumsiness does not offend me."

Ji Yue exhaled a grateful breath in relief. She was not to be punished for hitting Bo Tao. Now she had to capitalize on her opportunity. She had to think of something clever to say, and she had to do it without looking at Bo Tao, without thinking of what they had done together and without wondering about what he was thinking and feeling right at that moment.

Fortunately, she had an easy topic at hand. "The news of the Taiping defeat is most excellent! I am breathless to see your plans for the northern lands such that no upstart can rise again."

It worked! The emperor's attention had been wandering to Li Fei, but at her words, he focused back on her. "Whatever do you mean?"

Ji Yue straightened, uncomfortable at his curt tone. "Only that when servants—or peasants—act badly, there is usually an underlying cause. Address that cause, and the meals once again appear hot and on time."

The emperor frowned at her. His face darkened, and his eyes grew cold. "Do you hear that, Bo Tao? Comparing our glorious empire to servants and meals!" He raised his voice so that all would hear. "Bad servants will be whipped. Upstart peasants who dare challenge the Dragon Throne will be killed. And that is the end of it!"

Cheers and claps greeted his rousing statement. Then he turned back to her, his humor restored. "But I like your butterfly pin," he added.

She could barely murmur a thank-you before he laughed again and strode back to his table at the front of the room. Sun Bo Tao lingered a moment longer, his gaze dark and uncertain on her. She met his look—she couldn't help herself—but she couldn't read his meaning. She merely felt that tension again, that low lute string that seemed to tighten between them whenever they saw each other. And then he was gone, his long strides easily catching up to the emperor.

"You have disgraced us!" someone hissed.

Ji Yue turned and was startled to see her fellow virgins glaring at her. "What?"

"He came to our table to talk with us, and you coughed all over him. It is no wonder that he rushed away. He must fear a plague from you!"

Ji Yue blinked. "What?"

"He will think we are like you! He will think we keep company with upstart women who challenge his authority!"

"I did no such thing!" she cried.

"You do it even now! Oh, we are ruined because of you!"

Ji Yue looked from face to face. She had just spent a delightful two hours at the banquet with these girls. They had laughed together and shared stories of their homes. And now each one spit into their napkins at her and turned their faces away. Even Li Fei would not look at her.

"My chances are my own," she finally said. "They will not affect yours."

"Ugly and stupid," Fan Mei Lin said. "She will bring us all down with her."

Ji Yue said nothing. Their minds could not be swayed, and worse, she feared they were right. Men's minds did not always remember details. The emperor might very well attribute her actions to one of them, but she doubted it. Especially since each girl would take pains to remind the emperor that it was Ji Yue who had insulted him so.

No one would remember that she had tried to compliment his statecraft, not insult it. He would only know that she had created discord in his home, and that was a sin that could never be forgiven, especially in the Forbidden City. In short, she had not only failed to impress the emperor but had turned every virgin against her.

7

JI YUE'S MISERY had only begun at dinner. When the banquet was over, the girls filed silently back to the virgins' palace. The moment the door was shut, they rounded on her. While the girls at her table hated her for spoiling their chances with her miserable actions, the others were angry that the emperor had spent time with "a dirty pig like her!"

Nothing about her was sacred. Her body, her hair, her smell were all fodder for insult. For one insane moment she thought the eunuchs might help keep the rancor under control, but to her dismay, they merely egged the virgins on. This was their entertainment. Plus, they had no wish for the bitterness to be turned back on them.

In the end, Ji Yue stopped defending herself. No one wished to hear her side, anyway, and she was too miserable to try to speak reasonably to anyone, much less the shrews that surrounded her. She simply wanted to go to her bed and cry herself to sleep. But she was blocked on all sides. No one would let her pass out of the main room. She had to wait it out, doing her best to ignore every hateful word.

But then someone recalled that the emperor liked her hairpin. Another screeched that the pin was hers and she ran at Ji Yue, her claws extended to regain her property. She succeeded. She ripped out the butterfly pin and took a handful of cemented hair as well.

The pain shredded the last of Ji Yue's patience. She had two brothers, she knew how to fight. So she grabbed the girl's arm with one hand and balled the other into a fist, slamming it into the girl's stomach. Her attacker crumpled to her knees, but the hairpin was still gripped tight in her fist. "That was my great-grandmother's!" Ji Yue said, and she went to pry it out of the shrew's fingers. She'd just managed to grab hold of one tiny wing when the first blow fell.

Clearly, someone else had brothers. A hard, compact fist slammed into her side. As Ji Yue began to drop, she saw a small foot in a bright red shoe fly toward her face. She twisted, taking the impact on her shoulders, but that only exposed her face on the other side. Blows began to rain down. She had no idea who attacked her, only why. Tonight she was the scapegoat for everyone's frustrations. As blow after blow fell, each more vicious than the last, Ji Yue could only curl into herself and pray. Surely it would end soon.

He saved her. Somehow she knew it would be him. Not the emperor, as she might dream, but the man who plagued her awake and asleep: Sun Bo Tao, Master of the Festival. She heard his voice, a deep, angry bellow that cut through all the high screeches.

She felt no more blows, only a dull ache from head to toe. The pain would grow worse later, but she already knew that nothing had been broken. The girls had been intent on a beating, not murder. The master was still bellowing, and she heard the noise of people withdrawing. Then she felt his hands, large but oh so gentle, on her back.

"Where are you hurt, Ji Yue? You must tell me. I cannot help otherwise."

Deep in her spirit, she wanted to answer. She'd never had a sister, and she had naively believed that some of her fellow virgins would be her friends. She was a foolish, foolish woman to have thought such a thing. She knew that now.

"Chen Ji Yue, you must answer me!" His voice held a tinge of panic, so she opened her eyes to look at him.

"Once many years ago," she said, "I was climbing to reach something I was not supposed to have." She blinked away her tears. With his help, she began to uncurl, wincing as she moved. "I don't remember what it was. A sweet perhaps or, more likely, my father's brushes. But it was too high and I was too small, so I fell and broke my arm."

"Ji Yue, where are you hurt?" He brushed his thumb across her cheek and it came away smeared with white paint and black charcoal.

"The pain was unbearable," she said, retreating to the memory of her mother's arms wrapped about her, and her father's voice, high and threaded with panic. "I screamed until my throat hurt as much as my arm, and still I did not stop."

"Ji Yue…" he murmured, clearly frustrated. He was running his hands down her body—her arms and her ribs, then her legs. There was nothing familiar in his touch, simply a quick pat everywhere to check for breaks.

She leaned forward and touched his arm before he reached her big feet. "This was a beating," she said. "Nothing more."

He froze. "I have already summoned the women's doctor."

She shook her head. She did not want to see that woman again or go into her examination room. "Send her away. I would know if something inside were broken."

He shook his head. "Not always," he said grimly as he handed her a cloth for her face. "Have you been beaten before?"

She wiped the worst of the paint from her face then pulled the now broken board from her hair. "Once by my father for practicing my brush strokes upon his fine paper. And once by my brother's tutor for doing his homework for him."

He frowned. "You did your brother's homework?"

She shrugged, then immediately stopped. Already her back was beginning to swell. "I was bored. And I didn't think the runt would claim my work as his own."

He smiled. This close, she could see the way his brow puckered when he was worried, and how his smile smoothed the furrows away. "Can you stand?"

She nodded. He gripped her hand, but there was something between their palms. He pulled back and turned her hand over. The mangled butterfly hairpin lay in her palm. She had ripped it back from the lying bitch who'd stolen it.

"I am sorry," he said. "It was a pretty piece."

It was mutilated beyond repair. The jade stones were broken or missing and the gold wire was twisted. She looked at the misshapen thing in her palm and something inside her broke. She began to cry, and once the tears began, they would not stop.

He tried to speak to her. She couldn't understand the words, but she heard his tone. He sounded much like her father had that day long ago when she'd broken her arm: alarmed, anxious and completely uncertain what to do. In the end, Bo Tao simply swept her legs out from under her and carried her from the virgins' palace. She didn't know where he was taking her, and frankly she didn't care. His arms were larger than her father's, his voice was deeper than her father's, but the comfort was the same. His touch was just as tender, and she wanted nothing more than to be held by him forever.

Then he stopped walking. He stood still for a moment while she listened to the steady beat of his heart. She liked the regular rise and fall of his broad chest. Then he eased down on a bench, gently resting her on his lap.

"We are alone now," he said. "You can cry as much as you like."

She smiled and wished she could rub her face against the skin on his neck, but his collar prevented it. "I am done crying," she said, her voice raw. Instead, her mind was consumed by the feel of his arms, the warmth of his body and the strength that surrounded her so completely that she thought she could never be harmed again. "Don't leave me yet."

He tightened his grip around her. "Are you sure you don't need to see the physician?" he asked. With her ear pressed to his chest, his voice was a deep, echoing rumble like the sound of thunder in the distance.

"I am fine so long as you hold me."

He didn't answer, except to lean back enough to settle her even more deeply into his arms. She smiled, happy to think of nothing beyond him. But that thought led to others. Her heart beat harder, and she remembered another time when his hands had been on her body, when his chest had been pressed tight to her back, and his hands...

"Where are we?" she asked by way of distraction. She knew they were in a bower of sorts. She could feel the breeze, but in the darkness, she could see little more than the stone bench upon which they sat.

"It is a garden near the emperor's palace."

She jerked in alarm. "But he cannot see me like this!"

His grip tightened on her, keeping her in place. "No one comes here at night but me. Certainly not Yi Zhen. And even if he did, we would hear him long before he could see us."

Reassured, she relaxed back against him, acutely aware of the way his thighs rippled as he adjusted to her. And of the burning heat pressed intimately against her. "But where is this place?"

"It is my aunt's garden. Well, not specifically hers, but she was the only one who tended it."

She frowned. "You have an aunt in the Forbidden City?"

He nodded. "She was part of Emperor Dao Guang's lowest harem. That is how I came to be friends with Yi Zhen. My mother was visiting her sister. One day I escaped them and found him."

Ji Yue smiled. "My brothers often ran away from me, as well." She straightened, intrigued by the idea of meeting one of Bo Tao's relatives. "May I meet your aunt tomorrow? I would love to talk with her. I like gardening, too, and would often help the workers when I was little."

He shook his head. "I'm sorry. My aunt was selected to be buried with the emperor."

She swallowed, understanding the harsh fate that sometimes awaited members of an imperial harem. Being buried alive with the emperor was one of the worst. Still, she spoke the words that were expected of her. "She was greatly honored."

Bo Tao grimaced. "I have never thought it much of an honor, but I know she believed it."

Ji Yue sighed, uneasy with the idea of what could very well be her own fate someday. "Did she... Was she awake in the tomb?"

"I hope not. I brought her poison sealed in a perfume bottle. She should have fallen asleep, then died quickly while at rest." He took a deep breath, and Ji Yue felt it shudder inside him. "I hope it went like that. We will never know if it did not."

"I'm sure it did. I'm sure she was very grateful."

His hands tightened on her, and she went where he silently urged her: back into his arms. She listened to the night birds and the whisper of the wind through the leaves. But mostly she felt the wildness building inside her again. Would he touch her like he had before? She shouldn't want him to, but she did. She should be aching for the emperor's caress, the emperor's hot press of body and groin, the emperor's...

"Are you feeling better?" he asked.

"Yes," she lied. In truth, she was beginning to feel an ache deep in her womb. It was shame. She was ashamed that her thoughts lingered on a very unvirginlike desire for the absolutely wrong man.

"Do you think you could walk? I have something I want to show you."

"Yes, of course." She reluctantly shifted out of his arms, standing carefully. Her clothing was torn in a dozen places and her hair constantly strayed into her eyes, but she didn't care. Despite the conflicting emotions inside her, this night had taken on a magical quality, and she did not want it to end even if she walked around in rags.

"It is not far, but it requires a little bit of climbing. I would not be able to carry you."

"I am fine," she repeated, her curiosity piqued.

With a nod, he gestured her out of the bower. They walked together in silence. He kept a hand on her back and another on her arm, leading her through the dark maze that was the Forbidden City. They ended at a ladder that led up a massive tree.

"It is up there," he whispered into her ear, "but I must empty it out first. Wait here in the shadows and don't make a sound."

She nodded her agreement. Within moments he disappeared up the ladder. Then to her shock, four eunuchs descended in rapid order. They went in the other direction, grumbling and laughing among themselves. Bo Tao descended a moment later.

"They are gone now," he said.

"What did you do?"

"I bribed them to leave. Now no one will know that you are here."

She stepped forward, looking up into the blackness above. "What if someone else comes?"

"They won't," he said as he placed her hands on the ladder. "There is a way to bar entrance to anyone else. Besides, the show is not that interesting tonight."

"Show?" she asked.

"Hush. Climb."

She did as he bid, though it was hard going. Her skirt was already ripped, so there was no difficulty there. But he placed his hands on either side of hers, and he mounted each rung directly behind her. When he bumped against her bottom or leaned close enough to heat her shoulders with his chest, she gasped at the contact and thought inappropriate things. What if she had not hit him in the examination room? What would have happened? With his body around hers and his hand exploring her, what would have happened? What would she have felt?

By the time she made it up to a platform at the very top, her mouth was dry and her breasts heavy. "What is it that you want me to see?" she asked, her voice thready in the darkness.

He didn't answer in words. Instead, he crawled beside her and gently twisted her shoulders around until she looked through an opening in the branches. From there she saw into a room in a palace. There were people inside—women—but what were they doing?

Bo Tao was still holding her to direct her attention. Now he leaned closer to whisper into her ear. "We are looking at the surviving harem of Dao Guang. This is a room in their palace."

"But what are they doing?"

"Can you not guess? Do you not understand?"

She did understand, but she had never thought to see three women in the throes of sexual congress.

"Do you know that women establish a hierarchy in a harem? That one is the head female and the others must follow her rules?"

She nodded. That was why the fighting was so vicious in the virgins' quarters. The hierarchy had yet to be established.

"That woman lying out on the floor is Tai Lai, the head of this harem. She has ordered the others to pleasure her."

Ji Yue blinked, leaning forward on her knees to see better. The woman on the ground seemed to be the oldest there. She lay on her back as one girl suckled her left breast and used her other hand to manipulate the nipple of the right. The second girl crouched at the groin, using her mouth to lick and stroke there. All three were naked.

"With no men to please them, the members of the harem delight themselves. Sometimes it is this way, with each other or with willing eunuchs. Sometimes it is in ways more cruel and bloody."

The moment of ecstasy was building inside Tai Lai. Her moans were growing louder and she began to thrash her head. The younger two intensified their efforts, holding her down when her movements became too vigorous. And then she arched her back, screaming out in her passion. Meanwhile, the other two leaned back, breathing hard themselves from their exertions.

"How long has this platform existed?" Ji Yue whispered. "She should know she is being observed."

"She knows," he said. "She is the one who commanded that it be built. It intensifies her pleasure to know that eunuchs watch her and mourn for what they have lost."

Ji Yue wanted to turn away, she wanted to look at Bo

Tao's face to judge if he lied. But she could not tear her eyes from the tableau before her. Tai Lai's recovery came quickly. Her breath returned to normal and she reached out to fondle the breasts of the nearest girl, pinching and pulling despite the younger one's winces. Except, of course, the girl did not seem to be in great pain. Her face became flushed and her hand slipped between her thighs to touch herself.

"But that must hurt!" Ji Yue said.

"It does. But in this place, pain and sex can become twisted together."

The girl was beginning to moan as her hand worked between her thighs. The other one—still crouched between Tai Lai's legs—began to stand, but Tai Lai shot her an angry look.

"Again!" she commanded. "Slower this time."

The other one nodded and bent to her work. And then there were two women moaning and thrashing while one made noisy slurps that carried through the night air.

"And this is how they entertain themselves at this hour?" Ji Yue asked. "While others watch?"

"At night and during the day sometimes. How else can they occupy their time with no children to care for and no man to ease their suffering."

"But surely when Dao Guang was alive—"

"This is the lowest harem. He never called for any of them. All of them are still virgins, all imprisoned in the Forbidden City, unable to leave even to visit their own families. Most are not told when their parents die. Their life is reduced to this palace and these spectacles."

She shuddered at the thought. "Surely not all do this."

"No. Only a few. Others spend their time in petty rivalries and cruel revenges. Many have turned to religion, a few to music and poetry. But I have seen as many as a dozen in that room, including eunuchs."

"And how many watched from here?" she asked, at last able to turn away from the sight.

His teeth flashed white as he grinned. "I feared for the tree that night, so many were perched here or had climbed into the branches."

Ji Yue didn't dare look into his face when she asked her next question. So she let her gaze drop to his corded neck while her fingers toyed with a rough tear in her skirt. "Have you ever joined the…the revelry in there?"

He shook his head. "I am a whole man. I would be killed were I to enter."

She looked up to see his face. There was a kind of mischief in his eyes and she knew the truth. "You have joined them there!" she accused.

He shook his head. "Never. I swear."

"But you have done something. You have the same look my brothers have when they have stolen tarts."

He grinned, his teeth flashing in the darkness. "I have been on this platform with women who are not protected virgins." He leaned forward and touched her face. His hand slipped down her cheek and then brushed across her nipple so that tingles shot through her body. Before she could do more than gasp, she felt his other hand glide up her thigh. The rips in her skirt gave him many places to touch, many places to burrow. She felt his hand curve around the top of her thigh to stroke against her curls.

"Have you ever experienced what those women do? Have you ever felt the tremors rack your body as you cry out in joy?"

She shook her head. Never had she done such things.

"You were so creamy before," he said as his hand slid

deeper between her legs. "Has seeing this made it so again? Do you even understand what I am asking?"

"No," she breathed, though she gave no power to the word because, of course, she did understand in part. Her thighs were wet, and her womb quivered in desire. And she had thought so much of these things, even before entering the Forbidden City. She had seen dogs in copulation, heard the moans from her parents' bedroom and even watched as servants met in secret in the back garden. So she did know some, and she wondered. She most especially wondered what it would be like to experience such a thing with him.

Behind them, the concubines' cries were reaching fever pitch. And in the darkness of their tree bower, Ji Yue let her legs spread the tiniest bit. Then a bit further as his fingers delved deeper.

It was the knuckle of his index finger, she believed, that pushed against her first. She gasped in shock and had to grip his shoulders to steady herself. But that lifted her higher up, which gave him more room as he stroked between her petals.

"Yes," he said, "I believe you have been using your cream again."

Blood roared in her ears, her entire body was on fire, but her attention was centered on the place where his long finger stroked, rolling ever so slowly from front to back. Every knuckle made her shiver, and she released a high keening sigh.

"No man has ever touched you like this?" he asked. "You have never done this to yourself?"

"Never," she gasped. If only she'd known what it felt like before. Her skin seemed to pulse and her body throbbed where he touched.

"Good," he said as he turned his hand over so that he cupped her fully. His hand was large and intimate, and she felt as if he held the whole of her in his palm. "Then you will remember me always," he said as he pushed a finger inside her.

She cried out in alarm. No man had ever penetrated her like that before. But it felt good. Wicked, but good. Then he withdrew, rolling his knuckles forward across a place she'd only discovered with him earlier that day.

"Move as you will," he murmured as he leaned forward to support her upper body better. "Make whatever sounds you like. They are common here."

She didn't want to act so wantonly. She knew this was not the behavior of a virgin, and yet how could she stop when his hand and body urged her to move? Her thighs tightened and she rose higher on her knees. Without her willing it so, her back began to arch, and her hips thrust forward and back, forward and back over his hand.

"So hot," he whispered. "So wet. I cannot believe you are a virgin."

"I've never—" she gasped, her mind splintering.

His fingers moved without pattern. Or perhaps she could not understand the pattern, for her mind was completely absorbed in the feel of his fingers on her body, the sweet thunder of her heart and the wildness he drew from her so effortlessly. She was shaking, her buttocks lifting and lowering her as he spoke encouragement. Chest to chest, he held her while he pressed his finger inside again, then pulled it out, pressed it in and pulled it out.

"Kiss me," he said against her ear. "Kiss me so you do not scream."

She had no strength to do anything, but he had power enough for them both. He pressed his mouth to hers and thrust his tongue inside. He explored every part of her mouth while still touching her rhythmically below. And then it happened.

She cried out, her mouth fused to his. She clenched her muscles, then contracted them. A bliss radiated through every inch of her, every pore. He held her as the contractions roared through her blood. He kept his mouth on hers, his hand cupping her and his finger deep inside, still thrusting into her. She felt him there as her body tightened around him and her mind splintered from the wonder of it all.

Such bliss!

And when the shudders eased, when the breath returned to her body and her thighs relaxed downward, he still held her tight, supporting her as she fell back onto her heels. He pressed tiny kisses to her cheek, then down her neck. His hand remained cupped against her body, his one finger still pressed deep inside her. She did not move to close her legs. She did not have the strength.

"That was wonderful," she whispered.

"There is more," he said.

She blinked. She could not imagine more. Then he lifted his head, his eyes twinkling in the darkness.

"Did you not hear Tai Lai?" he asked. "She said, 'Again. This time slower.'"

8

SHE DIDN'T UNDERSTAND! Bo Tao cursed himself for a fool, and not for the first time that day. Thinking back over the way he had stroked her again and again, he realized that Virgin Chen Ji Yue had been so caught up in the wonder of what they did, in the sensations flooding her body, that she'd never understood his message. And he had become hypnotized by watching her reach ecstasy time after time that he'd forgotten his original purpose.

He'd meant to show Ji Yue the horrible life of an imperial concubine. Most concubines never lost their virginity, never enjoyed family or children, never had anything of meaning in their lives. They were reduced to performing sex shows for their amusement. He'd wanted to show Ji Yue an empty future so that she could choose a different path now, before it was too late. She could leave the competition of her own volition. Instead, she hadn't heard and he'd become enraptured by the sight of her shattering in his arms. He'd forgotten everything but giving her pleasure, and so the message was lost.

What was the matter with him? Why could he not just take her and be done with it? He could have had her. More than once, most likely. Around her, his dragon organ was always ready for more. And then when he was done, he could have dropped a word to the dowager consort and Ji Yue would be expelled by morning. Easy. Unless, of course, the emperor found out. Then Bo Tao would be killed for daring to touch one of Yi Zhen's women.

So he had held off. He had walked Ji Yue back to the virgins' palace, ready to carry her again if her legs did not support her. He had kissed her once more as they hid deep in the shadows, then he'd turned away. Now he was heading to the emperor's palace with his root so thick he had trouble walking.

He'd tried to hide his affliction, but Yi Zhen noticed immediately. The emperor had been coming down the stairs, seen his friend, then started laughing so hard he gripped his sides from the pain. Bo Tao called his emperor an ass and then stormed off to the room he used when politics kept him too late in the Forbidden City to return home. His emperor followed, though, laughing with every step. But by the time they reached Bo Tao's bedroom, his eyes had gone deadly serious.

"They are *my* virgins, you know," the emperor said.

"I know," Bo Tao groused. "Why do you think I am like this?"

"Because you are a true friend and a loyal bannerman."

"Go fuck a dog," Bo Tao retorted, then he flopped down on his bed. Yi Zhen laughed again, but Bo Tao wasn't fooled. Yi Zhen did not like sharing. Those virgins—Chen Ji Yue included—were his, and Bo Tao would be smart to remember it. Otherwise, his life would end much too young.

Eventually the emperor grew tired of laughing at him and left him to sleep. Unfortunately, his affliction prevented that. So he lay in bed wondering what to do with a mouthy virgin who made him hornier than when he'd seen his first "harem show." She didn't understand, damn it! Did she really want the hideous life offered to a concubine? Of course not! No sane person would want to endure the constant backbiting, petty rivalries and outright danger of living in an imperial harem.

But he had never found much logic among the female

population. And though Ji Yue appeared more intelligent than most, she still hadn't heard his message. And he didn't know how he could make it more plain! So he thought and thought while at the same time remembering how she'd undulated over his hand. Passion made her throat flush and her breath short. And, oh, he ached for her.

But it wasn't until the earliest streaks of light touched the sky that he remembered something else. He recalled what she'd said to the emperor to begin this whole evening's debacle: something interesting about rebels and servants and the underlying cause of the revolt.

That intrigued him. He found it strangely perceptive, especially from a woman. Had she overheard someone say that? Maybe her father? Or had she thought of it on her own? He had to know, but he had to be subtle. It wouldn't do to bring more attention to himself or her.

He waited another hour until the sun rose, then went about his duties while surreptitiously searching for her. He found the women's doctor instead. He only now remembered that he had forgotten to dismiss her last night. He had summoned her for Ji Yue, but had never brought the girl in. One look at the physician forestalled his words of apology.

"You look exhausted," he said with shock. Then dismay blossomed in his heart. "Was there some emergency last night? Something I wasn't notified about?" *Something that happened while I was in a tree making an imperial virgin spill cream over and over again?*

Xie Yan glared at him. "Emergency?" she snapped. "No. Just endless complaint after stupid complaint. Was there a riot last night?"

He frowned. "They attacked Chen Ji Yue because the emperor complimented her hair pin."

The doctor rolled her eyes. "I did not see Chen Ji Yue. But I saw every other ridiculous scratch and bump these cosseted babies could think of. They miss their mothers!" she snapped. "Girls who wish to be empress should not miss their mothers!" She kept muttering as she stomped away from him. At the last moment she shot a glare over her shoulder. "I am going to bed. Do not call for me again unless someone is in childbirth."

He nodded. No chance of that, especially since the day would be spent discovering family histories and fortunate horoscopes. During the family history exam, the virgins would be questioned about their birth, their parentage, their parents' births and beyond. The information was never officially recorded, but he wished to be sure that no imposter accidentally became empress. As much as possible, their answers would be verified before any girl entered the final Festival of Fertility. With that thought in mind, he headed to the place where Chen Ji Yue recounted her lineage.

It took some time to find her. A dozen other tasks had to be dispatched before he arrived, but he was there for most of her recitation. She was indeed the person she claimed to be: Chen Ji Yue, the daughter of a red bannerman, the lowest of the aristocracy. She recited correctly the list of her father's, grandfather's and great-grandfather's accomplishments. She also knew the astrological fortunes of their births and deaths, their lives and that of all their sons.

When Bo Tao asked, she also recited the names of her mother, grandmothers and great-grandmothers, though the interrogator looked at Bo Tao strangely for the question. Bo Tao ignored him, stepping forward to ask more personal questions.

"Your father passed the civil service exam and now lives here in Peking as a legal advisor to the Dragon Throne?"

Ji Yue nodded. "He works very hard and is extremely loyal."

Bo Tao waved aside the standard words. "Have you ever assisted him with his work?"

Her expression turned wary. "What do you mean? I am a woman. How would I ever help my father?"

"But you do, don't you? And your mother, as well."

"Of course not!" she said with a shudder. "I would never do such a thing!"

She was lying. He was sure of it. But he couldn't press further with the interrogator in the room. With a slight bow of apology, he decided to make amends. "I had to ask, Chen Ji Yue. Your father's work is most brilliant." Another lie. Ji Yue's father was an acceptable lawyer, but not a great one.

Ji Yue was still affronted. "You cast aspersions on my father's good name! Such a suggestion could ruin him!" The fear in her tone was real, and he made another attempt at apology.

"Sometimes I ask groundless questions to see how a woman reacts. I swear to you, neither I nor Mr. Wu believes your father to be anything less than a most honest and loyal man of great capability." He glanced at the inquisitor. "Is that not true, Mr. Wu?"

The man nodded, his eyes huge. Bo Tao made a mental note to step into a few more interrogations and ask ridiculous questions just to cover his tracks. He straightened and smiled genially at Ji Yue. "The questioning is done. Thank you, Mr. Wu," he said to the inquisitor. "I am sure you would like a break now. Go to the kitchens and ask for some tea. I believe they are making fresh pork bao this morning."

The man's eyes lightened and he rose quickly. Mr. Wu was known to be a great lover of pork bao. Ji Yue rose, as well, bowing to them both as she started to withdraw. Then Bo Tao snapped his finger.

"One moment please, Chen Ji Yue. The head eunuch wished something from you. What was it?" Then he made a show of trying to remember while the interrogator grabbed his coat and departed, his long queue whipping behind him in his haste.

The moment the door shut behind him, Bo Tao's expression turned harder. "The truth now, Ji Yue. I swear I will not harm your father in any way, but I must know the truth. You and your mother help him, do you not?"

Ji Yue flushed. "No!"

"Do not lie to me!" He did not shout the words, but released them as a low growl. He had found that to be much more effective than bellowing, and it worked on Ji Yue. Her eyes widened and she bit her lip.

"My father is a brilliant man!"

"Of course he is," Bo Tao soothed. "But no man can do the volume of work that he accomplishes. Someone must help him."

Ji Yue squirmed. "Sometimes my father's hand cramps. I write as he dictates."

"And your mother?"

She bit her lip. "The same."

Just as he suspected. "How many of the Confucian texts have you read?"

She blinked. "It is helpful to understand the context of what he dictates."

"How many?"

"All."

He began listing off all the texts required in a man's education. She had read half and was familiar with all. Then he leaned forward, his eyes narrowing in thought. "If you were a man…" He let his voice trail away suggestively.

"But I'm not," she said with some bitterness. "I am a

woman." She raised her eyes to meet his directly. "I am a woman who can help a man who lives and breathes politics. I am a woman who understands his frustrations even as she soothes his weary body. I will bear his sons and listen to his problems." She straightened to her full height. "I will make an excellent empress."

He swallowed down a surge of fury at her words. It wasn't rational, and so he suppressed it, but it made his voice hard. "The emperor could not acknowledge your words last night. No woman should dare to question his rule."

"I was trying to make an impression," she snapped.

"You succeeded." Then he folded his arms. "You said he must look to the underlying cause of the rebellion. The Dragon Throne needs to know—what did you mean by that? What cause do you see beneath the Taiping uprising?"

Her eyes turned pensive, but when she spoke, he heard conviction in every word. "My father is honest and so we are poor. Even for a lowly lawyer, bribes are rampant. Surely as master of these festivities, you know of what I speak."

He grimaced. Of course he knew. As China grew, so did the layers of bureaucracy. And where there were bureaucrats, there was the tendency toward graft.

"My father values his integrity more than his wealth, but others are not so wholesome." She shifted, then abruptly stepped forward in her earnestness. "The peasants follow two things: food and hope. Rebel leader Hong Xiu Quan offers both. Why doesn't the government offer its people something so simple? Why do the outlying governors give so little to the people they are sworn to protect?"

He felt his eyebrows rise in surprise. She obviously understood China's problems. "Does your father share your views?"

She snorted. "My father is a scholar. He buries himself in

texts that are hundreds of years old. It has not prepared him for a country threatened by rebellions and foreign powers."

"There have always been threats to China's sovereignty."

She nodded. "Did those threats have guns such as the white people carry?"

He shook his head, and his eyes grew pensive. "I saw a drawing once of an English gunboat. I do not know if the picture was real, but if it was…" He sighed. "I fear what will happen to China if the English become greedy."

She reached out and touched his hand, hope shining in her eyes. "You do understand. You agree with me!"

He nodded. "And China cannot weaken itself by fighting more rebels from within." The feel of her small hand on his warmed his spirit and stiffened his rod. But his mind was filled with other thoughts that miraculously directed him beyond taking her to bed. "I must go question the other girls. Since you have passed the family history exam, you must have a meal with the dowager consort." He slanted her a hard glance. "She will pick at you, but say nothing that is not…that is not…" How to phrase what he wanted?

"Empty headed?"

"Exactly! Pretend you will follow her direction blindly."

"She is not that stupid. She will not be fooled."

"Probably not, but she cannot be sure. After the meal, pretend you're ill. Claim you need to sit in my aunt's garden to rest." He used his finger to trace the route she would take from the garden lunch to the bower. If she could not remember it from his quick movements, then she was of no use to him.

"I understand," she murmured. "What then?"

"I will have someone there waiting. He will take you where I want you to go."

She nodded, but her eyes grew wary. "Do you swear on your honor that I will not be harmed by this?"

He winced. She was right to question him. Even now, his cock was large and hungry. "I swear by my honor that this will not hurt your chances to become empress." The words were sour in his mouth, but he said them anyway. If she would only give up her quest to become empress, then he could court her without fear from the emperor. He paused, momentarily shocked by his own thoughts. Did he plan to court her? To marry her? The idea was…not unappealing.

"And my father's reputation?" Ji Yue pressed.

"Was never in any danger from me." He smiled. "Though I would very much like to meet your mother. She sounds like a most interesting woman. Are your brothers as clever?"

"The youngest is. The older…" She hesitated.

"Takes after your father?"

"He spends much time in his dreams."

Bo Tao laughed and pushed to his feet. He had a moment's insanity when he dreamed he would pull her into his arms. Her breasts were within reach, and her sweet cream flowed so easily. But the interrogator would return any moment now, and after last night's warning from Yi Zhen, he had to be doubly careful. "Go now," he said as he pushed her away. "Go quickly."

She hesitated just a moment, and her eyes lingered on his mouth. He knew she was thinking as he was, that she remembered every detail of their intimacy, and the lust that surged through him nearly overpowered his reason.

"Go!" he rasped.

She nodded and fled.

9

JI YUE WAITED IN THE GARDEN, fidgeting with her clothing. Lunch with the dowager consort had gone exactly as predicted. Fortunately Ji Yue had kept her head. No matter how the woman picked, Ji Yue had responded with her most insipid thought. It went against the grain, especially since every answer made the dowager consort even more angry. It rarely helped to make the head female upset, but Ji Yue put her faith in Bo Tao's advice and remained as stupid as a bowl of rice.

But the longer Ji Yue waited in the garden, the more she doubted her sanity. Why would she put her faith in a man who clearly disregarded every rule of proper conduct? He had climbed into her palanquin, he had taken her last night to a place that no decent woman should ever see, and the things he had done to her!

Her face heated, but not with shame. The things they had done had been incredible, and she desperately longed to do them again. Then she shivered in true fear. He was teaching her the delights of physical congress. What if she did not become the empress? What if the emperor was *not* a frequent visitor to her bedroom or, worse, not even remotely as skilled as Bo Tao? Would she end up like those women in the dead emperor's harem? Would she stretch herself out for all to see while she ordered someone to pleasure her?

The thought was horrifying, but it was also a real possibility. Having tasted ecstasy with Bo Tao, she wanted more. She wanted a lot more. Thankfully, she was saved from further thoughts as a young eunuch approached, bowing deeply before her.

"Chen Ji Yue? Are you ill?"

She nodded and pressed a silk handkerchief to her lips.

"Sun Bo Tao worries for your health and asks that you follow me. He has found some medicine to strengthen your health for the festival ahead."

She nodded and smiled. "I would be most grateful."

She started to move, but he pressed a cloak into her hands. "The sun might damage your skin and make you feel worse, Chen Ji Yue. Perhaps this would help."

She frowned and wrinkled her nose at the perfume stench that rose from the cheap garment. It was the kind of thing that merchant wives wore or… She swallowed. Or prostitutes. He was dressing her as a prostitute.

At her hesitation, the eunuch nodded again. "Many women come and go in these garments, and no one sees."

No one was trained to see the whores who visited, he meant. Clearly the emperor and his friends had a regular habit of entertaining such ladies. And just as clearly, she would be safer moving about the Forbidden City in one of these cloaks than as Virgin Chen Ji Yue.

With a reluctant grimace, she drew the cloak around her and covered her head. Then she followed the eunuch through what seemed to be little-used pathways behind and around buildings. She saw workers—eunuchs and servants of all kinds—but no dignitaries and none of the other virgins. And though she peered from under her hood at the washer women and eunuchs, all cast their eyes discreetly away from her.

Until one woman did notice her. An older woman—a concubine by the looks of her gown—spat and cursed the whore that polluted the emperor. Her words were loud and vicious, and an ugly reminder of what would happen to Ji Yue if she lost her virgin status.

As a disgraced virgin, she could not go home. Even if her parents wanted her, it would damage her father's honor so much that he would not get further work. Certainly nothing from the imperial court. Without that income, the entire family would starve.

So if she could not go home, she would be forced onto the street with only one way to survive. From pampered aristocrat to street whore in one fatal step. She could not do such a thing. She wouldn't! She would strip off this hateful cloak and return to the virgins' palace and pray that no one noticed her absence. She would—

"Inside here, please," said the eunuch indicating a doorway.

Ji Yue frowned. "What is to happen—"

"Please," the eunuch whispered, his eyes darting around. There were men talking somewhere down the hall, and from their deep voices, Ji Yue knew they were not eunuchs.

She slipped into the darkness. The door shut behind her, and she shivered at the now total lack of light. A flint sparked. Sharp and bright, it lit a single candle wick. The light grew steadily, expanding its glow until she saw Sun Bo Tao, his angled features looking like stroked gold.

She stepped forward, relief making her breath loud. His eyes widened and he quickly pressed a finger to his mouth. She abruptly stilled. With the candlelight, she was able to see more. Bo Tao stood next to a writing table on which rested brush, ink stone and paper. Then he raised the flame higher. The room was tiny, with no decoration at all, but she could hear echoing noises from the near wall. It felt as if a great room stood on the other side.

Bo Tao came close, snaked an arm around her waist and pulled her tight. Her mind trembled in fear, but her body went willingly into his arms. And then he leaned close to whisper into her ear.

"I meet with a Dutch envoy today. Can you speak their language?"

She shook her head no. "But I have seen a Dutch child's book," she whispered. "I think I can learn their language."

"Excellent," he breathed, truly sounding pleased, "but of no help today. There will be a translator, in any event. I wish you to listen to our conversation and record it as best you can. But you must do so without candlelight."

She smiled. "My memory is excellent. It is how I have learned so much from helping my father."

His grip on her waist tightened in approval. Then he guided her to the wall, lifting her hand until she touched a latch over a bamboo shutter. "Extinguish the light, then open this shutter," he said. "There are peepholes in the tapestry. Listen and look, but do not make the tapestry move!"

"My mother does this behind the women's screen for my father."

He grinned as he turned back to her. "Your father was most wise in his choice of bride."

She smiled, flushing in pleasure. Most men would roundly damn her father for allowing a woman into men's affairs. That he understood her mother's value made her blood flush hot. Then all thoughts of her parents fled as Bo Tao tightened his hold on her.

"If you are discovered, I cannot help you. It would go worse for you if I claimed knowledge of your presence here."

She swallowed, beginning to understand what she risked in this. But she had never seen a white man before and was most anxious to view her first. Plus, when Bo Tao held her like this, when she felt the strength in his arms around her, she could think of nothing but staying close to him no matter what the cost.

"I will not disappoint you," she whispered.

"I know," he said as he dropped his forehead against hers. She could feel the tension grow in his body. This tight against her, she could feel his dragon organ push into her belly while her woman's petals grew moist. Never before had she felt so much, so fast.

He groaned, low in his throat. She heard the sound and echoed it as she lifted her mouth to his. His kiss was deep and possessive, but she had learned much last night. She knew how to toy with his tongue, to suck it deeper into her mouth, and to nip whenever possible at his lips.

His hands slipped to her bottom, cupping her there as he pulled her roughly against his groin. His thickness was hot and hard, but there were too many layers of clothing between them. Then his hands slid upward, over her breasts, pinching through the fabric. She rubbed her hands over his chest, slipping them beneath his court coat, but he had a tunic on below. No flesh, no access, only layers of silk over hardened muscle.

"No," he gasped as he abruptly broke away. "The emperor has noticed. He is watching me. And you," he added. "He watches you, as well. It is why the dowager consort hates you. She knows his interest is piqued."

Ji Yue froze and pulled slowly back, thoughts tumbling through her head like heavy stones. The dowager consort *hated* her? And the emperor *watched* her? The very idea was incredible. But if they saw her, if Emperor Xian Feng watched her, then being here was madness! She should leave immediately! And yet she did not stir from Bo Tao's arms. Why did she not leave?

She had no explanation except for lust. She wanted Bo Tao's lips on hers. She wanted his hand inside her body. And she wondered—oh, how she wondered—what it would be like to have his jade stalk planted deeply inside her.

"Do you want me to take you back to the virgins' palace right now?" he whispered. "We can stop this madness here."

"No," she whispered. "No, I want to…" She couldn't finish. No virgin could admit those things aloud. So she waved to the inkstone and brushes. "I want to be of help to you. I was raised to be a political wife, helping my husband in this manner."

He nodded. "Then so be it." He stepped away, moving quickly to the door. But then he paused, his expression earnest. "I am not a hanger-on, Ji Yue. I understand these foreigners as no other in China. One day, the emperor will make my position official. I will be the advisor on foreign affairs, perhaps an ambassador, but he likes having someone unofficial to meet with these people. Someone smart who can arrange things unofficially."

She smiled. "I am a woman. I understand how things can be arranged without the men *officially* knowing anything at all."

"Soon things will change for me. Perhaps very soon, but—"

"But not just yet," she said. "I understand."

Then their time was up. At his gesture, she extinguished the candle. He waited in the darkness a moment longer, and in that time she heard his breath exhale with such longing that tears sprang to her eyes. Except that it could not be true. She could not hear longing in a man's breath. Perhaps it was her own need that she felt, her own anguish.

He had not even left the room, and yet she ached for the

loss of him. Her body felt cold without him beside her. And her womb cried at its emptiness. She took a step forward to say…she didn't know what. But before she could form a word, he was gone. He slipped out of the room, leaving her alone.

It was just as well. Her thoughts were impure, her virginity in danger. She knew better than to think of anything but becoming an empress. Her mother had said she was not beautiful, so she needed to be smart. A smart woman would tuck her feelings away, put aside her memories as well as her wishes. She did it with a firmness that would please her ancestors.

Then she went to the shutter and pulled open the latch. Very soon, she would see a white man for the first time in her life. Would he look like a monkey, as she had heard? Would he truly have a stench like a pigpen in August? She could not wait to see.

But as her eyes scanned the receiving hall on the other side of the hidden room, she looked not for the white envoy but Sun Bo Tao. What would he say to the foreign devils? How would he treat their insolence? She held her breath in anticipation.

She didn't have to wait long. The Dutch group was ushered inside—six men in all. She took careful note of their attire. She knew that distinctions in color and insignia were important in China, so they could be equally vital to these foreigners. As they grumbled and argued in their strange tongue, she had time to make rough sketches of their faces and attitudes.

One was obviously their leader. His gestures were more refined, and he had a habit of stroking his beard or his coat lapels when he spoke. The others fawned upon him in subtle ways. They maintained their arrogance as all men must, but they kept their chins just a bit less pronounced and their eyes shifted left and right more often.

Then Bo Tao appeared. He was magnificent. From his

gestures to his sneering lip, he moved to impress. He brought his own retinue of underlings—double the Dutch envoys— and all bowed and scraped as Bo Tao sat in the throne chair. It was not the Dragon Throne, of course. This was a lesser hall, but Bo Tao wore the auspices of power with a majesty that must match the emperor himself. The sight of him stole her breath away.

The preliminaries had begun. A Dutch underling offered a gift: a metal timepiece, she thought, but it was hard to see. Bo Tao accepted it with casual neglect, waving it aside as merely his due. Tea and dumplings were served and the Dutch ate. Bo Tao did not. After a polite interval, the Dutch turned and began the true purpose of their meeting.

But then the oddest thing happened. The one who she thought led stepped back as if unimportant. The one who stepped forward was the man she thought most apelike with his dark curling hair and his wide nose. Surely this was a subordinate, but he spoke in their bizarre tongue, and a ship's captain translated his words into guttural, dockside Cantonese.

Bo Tao, of course, did not speak such dialect. It would be far beneath his dignity, but Ji Yue did. Her old nurse had been raised in Canton and used to sing songs in that tongue. While another translator changed the Cantonese words into Mandarin, Ji Yue wrote down both what was said in Cantonese and what was passed on to Bo Tao.

And so it went with negotiations back and forth until Ji Yue thought her hand would break from the strain. The Dutch wished for more treaty ports—cities on the ocean where they could sell their wares. Bo Tao refused. China had no interest in Dutch goods, he said. The envoys brought more delightful presents—strange fabrics of string woven in interesting patterns, crockery and machinery of bizarre colors and shapes.

How Ji Yue wanted to inspect them all, but from her angle, she could only see tiny sections.

Bo Tao yawned. Then with a sigh he glanced at the window and promised to discuss their proposal with the emperor, but he made no move to leave. At first Ji Yue did not understand why, but then his craftiness became obvious. The real gift had not yet been offered.

The ape-man came forward, and his eyes took on a gleam of arrogance. Ji Yue did not like his manner even though he obviously thought he was acting refined. At his gesture, two men came forward with a mediumsize chest. It was placed in the center of the room. Then the ape man crossed to it and with thick fingers he pulled open the lid.

Ji Yue craned her neck forward to see, then gasped in shock. She might be a cloistered virgin, but even she knew the brown powder called opium. It was a deadly drug that had been declared illegal in China nearly a hundred years ago. But even with the emperor's edict against it, the white were more and more overt in their attempts to addict the entire population to its evil. Her father knew of dozens of court officials who either smoked the drug themselves or profited from its illegal sales. Clearly the Dutch believed Bo Tao equally corrupt. Or they hoped that the new emperor would reverse his great-grandfather's edict. They were about to learn otherwise.

Bo Tao's reaction was immediate. He bellowed with rage, and every man in his retinue drew a sword. Ji Yue was hard put not to scream as the Dutch responded in kind. But they were too slow, and obviously Bo Tao had planned for this. Within seconds every foreigner had a blade at his throat.

Bo Tao's nearest assistant stepped out from his position beside the throne. While Bo Tao sat with regal disdain, his man stomped over to the chest and spat in it. He spoke not a word, but his meaning was clear. Opium was not wanted in China.

Two blades trapped the ape-man, one on either side of his neck. Already a trickle of blood oozed down his throat. The ape-man was purple with rage, but he didn't dare move. The assistant walked directly in front of the man and raised a long dagger, setting it carefully—point upward—just beneath the bearded chin. A slight push, and the ape-man would be dead.

Apparently the man knew it, too, because he began to babble in Cantonese, pleading for his life and offering all sorts of gold and jewels in trade. Bo Tao's translator didn't say a word, not even bothering with a man's dying words.

Ji Yue barely remembered to keep writing. She knew her calligraphy would be hideous because she could not shift her gaze from the tableau before her.

Then the assistant moved again. With a flick of his wrist—faster than she could see—he cut a mark like a dragon in the ape-man's cheek. Back on the throne, Bo Tao clapped his hands twice. The sound was so loud that Ji Yue would swear it echoed for minutes afterward.

More eunuchs came in. They poured an oil of some sort on the chest. The stench was so terrible that Ji Yue's eyes watered, and still the Dutch were held immobile by Chinese swords. In fact, all were frozen in place for a long minute.

Finally, when Ji Yue felt she would go mad from the strain, Bo Tao slowly stood up from the throne. If Ji Yue thought he was magnificent before, it was nothing to the power that radiated from him now. He walked like a furious god! He came down from the dais and moved coldly through the sea of swords. He walked straight up to the man whom Ji Yue had thought was the true leader. He stepped before that man and spoke clearly.

"Hear my words from the Dragon Throne. All who deal in that dung powder will be killed." He waited as his words went through both translators. He waited and he watched until the Dutch man dipped his head in acknowledgment.

Bo Tao did no more than blink, but suddenly, all the Chinese swords were sheathed. Every soldier stepped back while the Dutch remained awkwardly frozen in the center of the room. Ji Yue heard their shuddering breaths of relief, and yet none of them dared move beyond that. Meanwhile, the chest of opium was lifted by two eunuchs, tossed into the massive fireplace, and set on fire.

The ape-man scowled as the flames burst higher. The oily stench in the air made Ji Yue draw back, and she was pleased that a tapestry shielded her from most of the thick air.

Then the ape-man cursed. Ji Yue could not hear the words clearly for he muttered them, but it was a phrase she recognized. Her old nurse had used it when only the most vulgar of names would do. They were the last words he ever spoke.

Bo Tao whipped around and threw his dagger straight through the ape-man's thick neck. The man gurgled once, his eyes bulging in shock, then he fell forward, dead.

Ji Yue pressed a hand to her mouth to hold back her scream. The brush fell from her hand and she pulled back from her peephole. For a time, she did not think she could breathe. Even worse, she could not close her eyes because whenever she did, she saw the point of Bo Tao's dagger sticking out from the front of the ape-man's throat. She saw the blood welling and…

Ji Yue bit her lip. She would not scream. She would perform her duties as a good wife should. She would think of nothing else but her task. She had to record…nothing. Nothing else was said. Bo Tao stomped out of the room, but the soldiers remained. And the foreigners meekly gathered up the corpse and filed away.

Ji Yue waited, watching, while inside she shook like a leaf in a storm. Sometime later—she didn't even know how long—someone entered her tiny room. She didn't have the presence of mind to see who it was. But the moment his arms came around her, she turned and pressed her face into Bo Tao's coat.

"I'm sorry," he murmured. "I am so sorry. I did not mean for you to see that, but I could not allow such a slight from that man. Fear must be lasting and his had already faded. We are in such danger from their opium, you cannot know what I fear for our country."

"I know," she said as she lifted her mouth to his neck. "I know."

"You were very brave," he said.

She released a short laugh. "I was safely hidden. You were the man walking among swords."

"My men are very well trained. There was no danger to me."

She shook her head, easing away from him to make sure he saw her earnestness. "You are wrong, Sun Bo Tao. There is always danger with those men. They may be frightened now with your swords at their throat, but it will not last long. They will return."

Bo Tao's expression turned even more grim. "I know. China will soon be beset on all sides."

There was nothing she could say to that. He had confirmed her worst fears. But then he pressed a kiss to her forehead. "Come, come. Let me see what you have recorded."

"I have not finished," she said as she reluctantly pulled from his arms. "Mama taught me to write down my impressions after it was all done."

"Excellent advice," he said as he scanned her paper. Then his eyes suddenly lit with surprise. "You speak Cantonese?"

She nodded. "Mama was appalled, but I learned it from my nurse."

"In this, your mother and I disagree. A knowledge of the shippers' tongue is most valuable. Most valuable indeed!"

Then he sat down at the table to read her notes more directly. She hadn't noticed until then that he'd lit the candle, so she quickly shut the bamboo shutter.

"Sit, sit," he said as he gestured to the chair. "Write down your notes as your mama said, and then I have a surprise for you."

10

WHAT A POWERFUL WOMAN! Bo Tao thought as he watched Ji Yue's tiny mother inspect her daughter from head to toe. That had been his surprise for Ji Yue. Once she finished with her notations on his meeting with the Dutch, he'd escorted her to another room where her family waited. It had given him such joy to hear her squeal with delight and rush forward. The happiness she expressed when surrounded by her family went a long way to restoring his peaceful spirit after his disastrous afternoon.

The emperor would applaud his show of strength to the Dutch, but murder was never something Bo Tao would stomach with ease. That Ji Yue had witnessed his moment of violence disturbed him, but she'd handled it with more aplomb than two of his soldiers. They had to leave early to cast up their stomachs; she had sat quietly and recorded her notes. Looking at the mother now, he understood how the daughter became the amazing woman she was. Her mother would have tolerated nothing less!

But whereas the mother was almost shrewish with her tight words and pursed lips, Ji Yue was sweet-tempered and kind. Those must be the traits she got from her father, who was indeed rather vague in his mannerisms. Even the sons were just as Ji Yue described, the eldest lost in his own thoughts while the youngest missed nothing. But no one in this family could match the mother for power.

Bo Tao ordered food, then sat back and watched the family interact. He drank his tea and listened in silence as Ji Yue related a severely edited version of all that had occurred so far in the contest. They all cheered in delight that she had passed both the physical exam and the family history exam, which meant she had only the artistic display before the final selection. Then, just when he was at his most relaxed, the mother pinned him with her stare.

"This is most lovely, Sun Bo Tao. Our family can never repay such a kindness. But I cannot help but wonder if all the imperial virgins have family visiting. If so, then the Forbidden City must be overrun with happiness today!"

"Today has indeed been a happy day," he lied. "But no," he said, answering her unspoken question, "the other virgins have not been so fortunate as your daughter. They rest in the virgins' palace without the blessed kisses of their mothers."

Madame Chen's brows shot high. Or rather, they would have if the woman still possessed eyebrows. "Sweet heaven, we are richly blessed," she cried. "Has something occurred that we receive such beneficence? Ji Yue, what have you done to be singled out so?"

Ji Yue blushed a bright red. Damn. Such a shrewd woman would see right through any lie.

"It is a trifle, Mama. It appears I have gained the attention of the emperor."

"Really?" her mother said, hope and surprise at war on her features. "How?"

Bo Tao stepped forward. "A simple matter of translation, Madame Chen. Your daughter speaks the sailors' dialect of Canton."

"That terrible nurse!" the woman spat. "Had I known earlier of her background—"

"It is a most fortunate stroke of luck. In thanks, the emperor has allowed you to visit. All the girls miss their mothers."

"Pah," the woman said. "She is a grown woman and should be a mother herself."

"Exactly," Bo Tao agreed. And then he made his play, praying that the mother would think of more than simple politics. "Unfortunately, of the girls still here, most will never have a child. Most, in fact, will never even see the emperor except at a distance. I would shudder should such a sad fate befall your daughter."

Madame Chen shrugged. "That is the nature of things in the Forbidden City." Then she smiled and patted her daughter's hand. "But if you have already caught the emperor's eye, you have little to fear."

Bo Tao cursed silently. This was not going as he planned. He had hoped that the mother would understand what a horrible future was in store for Ji Yue. Clearly, Madame Chen only saw political opportunity. But maybe he could convince Ji Yue. He turned to her, wishing he could be more plain.

"Chen Ji Yue, you are a beautiful, talented flower of China. You have seen the rancor that is part of daily life here. You could return home now with your family—"

"Leave the Forbidden City?" gasped her mother.

Bo Tao glared at the woman. Could she not listen for a moment? Could she not see her daughter's fate rather than politics and opportunity? He glanced at the husband for help but saw that his eyes had gone vague like his eldest son's. Bo Tao doubted the man really listened.

"There will be more suitors for you, Chen Ji Yue. Why be one of thirty women when you could be first wife to one man?"

"No!" the mother cried before Ji Yue could speak. "Everyone knows that you came here, my child. We hired weepers! You cannot return home without every man wondering why!" She cast a canny look in his direction. "Why do you suggest such a thing to my daughter? Have you made her unfit somehow? A disgrace to her family which you wish to cover?"

Three curses upon the woman's head! There was no way to answer that honestly. "Your daughter is an imperial virgin," he snapped. "I believe she could make an excellent empress, but the dowager consort does not like her."

"Of course not! No mother wants to lose her place in her son's eyes."

Bo Tao grimaced. If only he had more time to explain! But any moment now, someone was going to summon him to the emperor to explain what had happened with the Dutch. He could not tarry much longer.

"You must see, Chen Ji Yue, what lies before you." He had shown it to her so plainly last night. Did she want to become one of the lowest harem women? "Leave now and I will find some reason. You are with your family. There will be no questions, certainly none that could not be verified by a doctor."

There it was as plain as he could make it. If she withdrew now, after a suitable period of time, he could begin a formal courtship. He would have to be sure that the emperor bore no ill will. But if Ji Yue became suddenly ill—so ill that she had to be returned to the bosom of her family—then perhaps the emperor would not guess. Or better yet, Yi Zhen might forget one virgin out of so many. There were hundreds of things that occupied an emperor's attention. It only required that Ji Yue say yes. Yes, she would willingly withdraw herself from the Forbidden City.

He looked into her eyes. He saw the uncertainty there. Another push and she would fall, he was sure of it. But she wasn't given the chance. Madame Chen did a little pushing of her own, shoving Bo Tao backward and away from her daughter.

"I know you, Sun Bo Tao," she hissed. "I know you are not a scholar, you are not a soldier. You are not even rich. You are a friend to the emperor and so he lets you live off his bounty, and you are jealous of whatever he likes."

"Mama, that's not true," Ji Yue inserted, but her mother was not listening.

"The emperor has noticed you, daughter," she snapped. "And this man wants whatever the emperor has. So he convinces you to go home now so that we will be grateful when he courts you later." Madame Chen drew herself up to her full height. "We will not be grateful for the likes of you!"

Bo Tao did not answer. Her accusations had the ring of truth. Once, he had lived off his friendship with Yi Zhen, had followed the emperor around for the parties, the food and the women. But endless rounds of princely games grew tedious. He discovered he liked the business of nations, and he grew up. Now he was an integral part of the nation's government even though he had no official title.

He looked at Ji Yue, his heart in his eyes. "I have enough to live. And after the festival, Yi Zhen has promised me an appointment with a salary. Enough money to support a wife and—"

"Bah on promises!" Madame Chen gripped her daughter's arm and spun her around. "Hsst! You are smart, Ji Yue. Use your head." Madame Chen pointed a bony finger at him. "Beauty fades and grows old. Imperial promises come and go with the wind. You want nothing of this one!"

Ji Yue compressed her lips in annoyance. Bo Tao could tell she did not like having her mother tell her what she wanted. But without her mother's support, she could not go home.

"Mama, the dowager consort despises me."

"Because the emperor sees your worth."

"I do not think—"

"Enough," interrupted the father.

Bo Tao turned, startled to hear from the man. "Honored sir?" he said with a bow.

"My daughter has caught the emperor's eye. She will remain an imperial virgin." He lifted his chin. "There is no room for her at home." Then he gestured to his sons. "Come, sons, your studies await. You do not want to become a wastrel, dependant upon promises before you can take a wife." And with that, he waved his daughter a casual farewell and walked away.

His wife fell into step behind her sons. But at the door, she turned to glare at her daughter. "Ji Yue, go! Go to the virgins' palace and spend no more time with this wastrel!"

Ji Yue did not appear happy with her mother's advice, but it didn't matter. Without a home to return to, Ji Yue would remain in the Forbidden City and take her chances among fifty others to become the next empress.

Bo Tao sighed. He could kill a foreigner in the lesser great hall, but he could not win a girl away from her parents' ambition. "Do as your mother bids," he said. "I am late to report to the emperor." He clapped his hands twice very loudly and a pair of eunuchs appeared. "Escort Chen Ji Yue to the virgins' palace. I am late."

With a last bow to her mother, who still smirked in the doorway, he turned and left both the Chen women behind.

11

Bo Tao did not see a single virgin for the next two days. He completely ignored his duties as master of the festival and remained at his home in Peking. He focused on his reports to the emperor, on strategies to outwit rebels or invaders, on anything that would keep his mind completely away from Chen Ji Yue.

It didn't work. He found himself reading her notations on the Dutch envoy, remarking anew that she had a keen eye for detail and a clear head despite the horror she had witnessed. He read it a hundred times or more, hearing her voice in his head as he did, feeling the touch of her hand and the heat of her body. By the dawn of the third day, he was insane with want. His jade stalk felt like a heavy stone dragging his thoughts straight back to her.

It was ridiculous! She was just a woman. She could not possibly be as beautiful, as sweet, as brilliant as he remembered. He ground the heels of his hands against his eyes. He had to see her again. That much was obvious. He had to prove to himself that he'd built a fantasy in his head. So he stormed from his home, barged through the gate of the Forbidden City, and went in search of a virgin.

He could not find her. The virgins had spent the last two days practicing their talents—whatever they might be—so they could entertain the dowager consort during the artistic display exam. Some painted, others sang or danced and some wrote poetry. Each day had produced a display of some sort for the dowager consort. And each day, someone had been dismissed as unacceptable because of one trifling reason or another.

He had watched the list of unacceptable virgins closely, hoping to see Ji Yue's name. If the dowager consort dismissed her, then perhaps her family would relent. Perhaps they would accept her back, and he could court her after his appointment—whenever that came. But her name did not appear because—he now learned—she was set to dance before the dowager consort today.

And Bo Tao was set to meet with Han Du Yu, a minor dignitary of a small but wealthy province near Peking. He wanted to give the emperor gifts—bribes—so that his son would pass the civil service exam. It was a ridiculous meeting given to Bo Tao because the emperor could not waste his time on such stupidities. Neither Bo Tao nor the emperor had anything to do with who passed and who did not. But every year desperate parents tried to buy favor where there was none to give.

Bo Tao would have ducked the meeting completely, but Han Du Yu was rich. So rich that the emperor could not afford to slight him. Worse, Bo Tao had been thinking about what Ji Yue said. If peasants followed food and hope, then the emperor needed to know exactly how hungry and how hopeless his people were. Short of interviewing every man, woman and child who slopped pigs, he had to rely on the nobles who oversaw their lands. And here was a perfect opportunity to do just that.

Therefore, much as he wanted to see Ji Yue dance, he could not cancel. Which meant he had to sit and wait. And wait. Until finally the fat, pompous ass arrived carrying a huge ivory carving of one of the nine Immortals, a celestial being in Taoism.

Bo Tao stared at the ugly thing. Bribes needed to be small and secret, not ostentatiously large. And it wasn't even carved well! Forgoing diplomacy in favor of expedience, Bo Tao pushed the stupid present back to the idiot. "I have nothing to do with marking the exam, I have no influence there, and have no wish to waste your money. Please, take this back."

The man laughed heartily, thinking that Bo Tao was merely pretending to have no influence, pretending to be honest. The harder Bo Tao tried to convince him, the more entrenched the stupidity became. In the end, Bo Tao had no choice but to accept the ugly piece or they would be there dickering all day.

Then Bo Tao leaned forward, getting to the meat of what he wished to know. "Tell me, Han Du Yu, of the people you oversee. What do the peasants say? What do they want?"

Han Du Yu grinned and clapped his hands. "They sing the emperor's praises night and day."

Bo Tao grimaced. Time was passing and this idiot thought he wanted false platitudes. "When smoking tobacco, when drinking at night, what do they say? What do your peasants want?"

"More beer."

Bo Tao quieted. "So they are hungry?"

"Of course not! The people in Zun Hua are happy. They simply want more beer to toast to the emperor's good fortune." Han Du Yu leaned forward. "I hear the imperial virgins are most beautiful. Will I see them today, do you think?"

The thought of Han's piggy eyes looking at Ji Yue made Bo Tao's stomach turn. "They are not show girls to be paraded about."

Han sighed. "Of course, of course. Perhaps tomorrow night, then. I have a message for the head eunuch from his brother."

Bo Tao waved the comment away. He had no interest in this man's maneuvering, though this was the first he'd heard of the head eunuch having a brother. It didn't matter. "Do the peasants come to you for aid? For rulings or judgments?"

"Of course, of course! They love my rulings." He grinned. "They love me."

"And what are their petitions?"

"Oh, the usual peasant thing. One man stole another's ox. This boy killed that one's chicken. The round of complaints is endless."

And completely ignored, no doubt. Well, he now knew how Han Du Yu became so wealthy. A man this casual about administering his province would be easily swayed by bribes.

Bo Tao pushed to his feet. "Thank you for your time and your lovely gift," he said, though the words nearly choked him. "I will go directly to the emperor with this…thoughtful present." He hefted the huge item, wishing he could use it to clobber the man. Then Bo Tao left, not even bothering with any of the formalities. He had no time for ridiculousness and now he was walking around with an ugly ivory statue.

On sudden impulse, he changed his direction. He knew exactly where the emperor would be at this moment, and fortunately, it was not in a public place. He stomped his way to Yi Zhen's palace and pushed past the eunuchs there. Longtime friendship counted for something, even with an emperor, so Bo Tao was soon admitted.

"Well, hello, my friend!" the emperor said with a grin. "You look like you just ate something sour. And I hear that you are neglecting the virgins, as well." He gestured to a tray with sweet dumplings on it. "Please, avail yourself—"

"This is for you. Han Du Yu is an idiot, and I'll be damned if I listen to yet another virgin spat even for you."

Yi Zhen's brows drew together in anger. He was not used to such disrespect, even from his best friend. With a wave, he sent his eunuchs scurrying away, then he glared at the carving. "That thing is hideous."

"It is a bribe so you can fix the civil service exam."

"For which son?"

Bo Tao frowned. He'd forgotten that Han Du Yu had three sons. "He didn't even say."

"He is an idiot."

Bo Tao leaned forward, trying to impress his emperor with the importance of his next words. "He is a corrupt official and an idiot."

Yi Zhen threw up his hands and drawled, "Because that is so rare in China."

"Three hours from Peking on a fast horse. So close to you and filled with such corruption."

"His is an unimportant piece of land for all that it so close. And none there would dare rebel. We would hear of it too easily."

Bo Tao growled in his frustration. "You do not understand! If you countenance such blatant idiocy so close to you, then what is it like where you have fewer eyes? No wonder the Taiping caught us unaware. If you cannot control those close to home, then how can you imagine to rule the far reaches of your empire?"

It was a valid point, and he could see the message filter into his friend's mind. In the end, Yi Zhen sighed. "How much of an idiot?"

Bo Tao hefted the ugly carving. "This was his bribe."

"It looks like a badly made stone phallus."

Bo Tao twisted it around, his brows contracting as he saw what his emperor had. "No doubt that was the appeal."

Yi Zhen waved it away. "Go and see to your duties with the virgins."

For all that he wished to do just that, Bo Tao hesitated. "I cannot continue this way, Yi Zhen," he finally said. "I value what I do for you and for China, but I am a grown man. It is time I saw to my family name."

"You wish your appointment." It was not a question. "So you can have a wife."

Bo Tao nodded, though he did not miss the hard tone in Yi Zhen's voice.

"Very well. Complete your duties as master of the festival with honor, and I will see to your appointment."

Bo Tao nearly groaned. Another promise to be fulfilled after another delay. How many times had he heard these same words? Just one more task, and he would get an official title. Just one more month, one more something, and all his wishes would be fulfilled. Bo Tao no longer believed in his best friend's promises.

"Yi Zhen," he began. "What title do you offer—"

"Idiot!" Yi Zhen roared and abruptly pushed up from the table. "Do you see what I look at?" He gestured at the maps and the military reports strewn on the table before him. "Do you think the Taiping are finished? Why do you press me now? Get out! Get out!"

Bo Tao bowed, his life tasting like ashes in his mouth. But what were his options? His life was subject to his emperor's whim.

"And take that disgusting thing with you!" the emperor snapped, indicating the carving. "It's my gift to you in thanks for your great service!" Then he laughed with cruel humor as Bo Tao grabbed the thing and departed.

There was no time left. The dowager consort's entertainment was set to begin within moments. Still carrying the statue, he rushed through the twisting pathways of the Forbidden City to the dowager's main garden. He made it there barely in time. The servants were just now clearing away the meal. Immediately afterward, Ji Yue would dance.

He scanned the crowd of faces, not even bothering to smile. The dowager had her courtiers there plus all the remaining virgins—over three dozen at last count. Add in eunuchs and other servants, and the number of bodies crammed into the garden was daunting.

There! He spotted Ji Yue as she limped toward the center. She limped? Bo Tao stepped forward, his eyes narrowing as he searched her face. Even from this distance, he could tell her cheek was swollen beneath her paint. She likely had bruises or scratches in other places, as well. But why was she walking so oddly? Graceful one moment, then halting and jerky the next. And she was about to dance before the dowager? She would fail the artistic display and be expelled for sure!

This was exactly what he wanted! He slowed his step, knowing that all he needed to do was wait for the inevitable disaster. He could wait and watch her dreams be destroyed in a painful and humiliating display. He would stand back and watch Ji Yue be crushed and then released in the hopes that her parents would relent and accept her back into their home.

Just wait a few minutes more, he told himself. But he couldn't do it. Having just had his own hopes crushed, how could he visit such a thing on Ji Yue? He couldn't. Even if it meant that she stayed an imperial virgin and he never, ever had a chance to court her.

So he had to stop her performance, but how? She was already arranging herself in the opening position. Then she lifted her head and blinked, obviously trying to hold back tears. The sight of her face looking so brave and yet so tragic broke something deep inside him. He did not care the risk to his career if he singled her out; he had to stop this farce now!

"Chen Yi Jue!" he bellowed.

The excited chatter abruptly stopped. All looked at him in shock.

"Chen Yi Jue, you will come with me now!"

"But she was about to dance," groused one of the virgins. Bo Tao pinned the girl with his stare, while searching through his memory. It was Gao Hua Si—the spoiled roommate of the someone-spit-in-my-white-paste tantrum.

"Do you think I care for your women's entertainment? I was just interrupted from an important meeting with Han Du Yu. Why? For this?" He hefted the ugly statue. He curled his lip. "A gift from your parents, Chen Ji Yue."

Ji Yue had straightened, a look of horror on her face.

"You will come with me now. You will write a letter to your parents to tell them that the master of the festival does not accept bribes." He curled his lip at the offending item. "And certainly not ones this ugly."

It was a lie. He had, of course, been given hundreds of gifts from the virgins' families. All of them were dutifully cata-logued and passed over to Yi Zhen, who wished to know the nature of the family who sired his future empress. Had Bo Tao kept even a tenth of the gifts, he would have enough money to establish a proper household and find a wife. But Bo Tao had been honest and so he had nothing. Nothing to support a wife, nothing to impress Madame Chen. Nothing, that is, except this one hideous carving.

Meanwhile, the dowager consort narrowed her eyes and stood as she addressed him. "You must be thirsty, Sun Bo Tao, please join us. Have some tea. After the performance, I am sure Chen Ji Yue will have time to do whatever you wish."

So it was a planned expulsion. The dowager could not fail to see Ji Yue's condition. If she wished to spare the girl, then she would have allowed Bo Tao to whisk Ji Yue away. But she hadn't. Which meant that the dowager wanted a public excuse to eliminate her. Anything private could be recanted. The humiliation had to be public and therefore assured. Which meant that someone even more powerful must want Ji Yue to remain.

Bo Tao nearly groaned. The only one more powerful than the dowager consort was the emperor himself. Yi Zhen had clearly taken an interest in Ji Yue, if only to torture Bo Tao. Sweet heaven, women's politics gave him a headache! He sighed and spoke from the heart.

"Great Imperial Dowager Consort Kang Ci, I do not care! I do not have time to eat nor do I wish to tarry. Chen Ji Yue will be punished for her parents' hideous effrontery to myself and the Dragon Throne. And she will be punished now."

And with that he gestured widely with the phallic statue. People cleared a pathway before him, if only to avoid being hit by the heavy thing. At the opposite end of the path stood Ji Yue, tears escaping from her eyes and streaking her makeup. An ache welled up deep inside him. He hadn't wanted to cause such anguish in her, but he'd had no choice. With a last bow to the dowager consort, Bo Tao turned away, forcing Ji Yue to limp after him.

12

"MY PARENTS DID NOT SEND that ugly thing!" she snapped.

Bo Tao almost smiled. Trust Ji Yue to defend herself to the very end, for all that she was alone and vulnerable in his private office suite.

"What is wrong with you? Why do you limp?"

She flushed and looked away. "It is nothing." Then she abruptly spun back to him, her eyes blazing. "And if you really cared, you would have stopped it from happening two nights ago!"

He grimaced at the confirmation of his fears. "So the virgins have continued beating you."

She nodded. "I have brothers. I know how to fight back." Then she took a wobbling step forward. "But why do you allow it? They are vicious bitches!"

He shrugged. "It is a woman's life in the Forbidden City. Like hens and a pecking order. Eventually the hierarchy will be established, but for now—" he shook his head "—as long as the dowager consort despises you, you will stay on the bottom. If I were to interfere, it would only go harder on you."

She didn't answer. She knew it was true.

Then he gestured to the couch. "Come, come. Let us see your injuries. I will call the doctor and she will do what can be done."

Ji Yue crossed her arms over her chest. "Call no one. I know what is wrong. It will heal in time."

Bo Tao narrowed his eyes. He did not like the fact she kept these things from him. "Tell me what is the matter or I will call the doctor."

She balled her fists and glared at him. "It is nothing, I tell you! I am beaten and bruised."

He stifled a curse. "I should have been here. I should have guarded you better." Then he sighed. "You know I must see these injuries, Ji Yue. You cannot always know what will fester and what will not."

"But you cannot!" she cried.

"I can. I am master of the festival, and I will see how a virgin under my care was injured." He had thought that seeing her again would decrease his desire. That his lust would fade in the cold light of day, but it was not so. Now that he had her alone, he would not be denied her. Not on this most frustrating of days.

She understood what he meant. She knew and he could smell her excitement in the closed air of his tiny office. His dragon stiffened to painful intensity, but he did not move. He saw the fear in her eyes. Finally she shook her head. "Someone will know."

"The door is shut." Then on impulse, he dragged a heavy table in front of it, blocking anyone from entering. "Someone must hear you being punished, Ji Yue. Your screams of pain must be very loud as I beat you for frustrating me so."

She straightened. "You do not seem like a man who beats a woman."

"Ah, but who knows where lust will take a man?" He took her to the couch, setting cushions behind her back before she slowly sat. "The emperor knows I crave you like a sickness, Ji Yue." Her eyes brightened at that, but he paused to let the knowledge sink in. "He is testing my loyalty. He knows there is another physical examination in two days."

She nodded. "The final check for virginity before he selects his brides."

"If you remain a virgin despite our time together, despite my beating you now, then he will know lust cannot tempt me away from my duties to him." He took a deep breath and told her everything. "I pray it is his final test before he gives me an appointment."

Her expression turned serious. "Then what my mother said is true. You have no wealth of your own?"

"Not enough for a wife or a family. Barely enough to keep a modest home on my parents' land."

"You depend upon the emperor, then," she said. She reached out, touching his face with a tentative caress. "As do I, since my parents will not have me back."

He took her hand from his cheek, pulling it slowly to his lips, where he pressed a kiss into her palm. "My fortunes may change," he said. Then he gestured to the papers in his office. "I am working very hard to get an appointment and a salary, but…" He shook his head.

"Not soon enough. Not for my mother, at least." She took a deep breath. "Did you know that the dowager expelled the Luo girl this morning? We are now down to the final twenty-eight virgins."

The news hit him like a blow to the chest. He had not realized that all the extraneous girls had been culled. Every one that remained would be divided into one of Yi Zhen's harems. He could barely breathe for the pain of it. "You have been selected then. You will be a concubine." His heart broke to say the words. Six days ago, he hadn't even known she existed. Since that time, he had gone from despising her to lusting for her to maneuvering every way he could so that he could court her. All to no avail. "I can never have you, Ji Yue. I thought if you were expelled, if I stayed away and the others found a way to push you out…" He began to pace out his agitation. "But I couldn't stay away any longer. I couldn't watch you in pain, humiliated for all to see."

He looked into her eyes and saw tears glistening there. She understood what he was saying. She knew what he would offer her if he could. But she didn't speak, and so in her silence, he did the boldest, most dishonorable thing he'd ever done. He guided her hands to his groin. She did not fight him, but let him lead, and when her fingers touched the bulge in his pants, he nearly groaned at the feel of her slender fingers.

"But there is a way we can take what pleasure is left to us without risking your virginity."

Her eyes leaped back to his face. "Like the women in the old emperor's harem. You would put your mouth…" Her voice trailed away and her skin turned bright red.

"Yes. And you could do the same to me. If you wished."

She bit her lower lip, her small white teeth pulling at the pink flesh in a way that made his blood pound. "It is all we could ever have of each other," she said softly. She put a hand on his chest to stop his agitated movements and looked up at him with dark, yearning eyes. "And besides, you could teach me what to do."

His heart was pounding from her touch, but his mind was still locked on the impossibility of his life. To finally find a jewel such as Ji Yue, and then be forced to surrender her to the emperor. "I cannot think of you in the lowest harem," he whispered. "Such a waste of your talents! Such a terrible life!"

She nodded and stepped closer into his arms. "Then you must help me see that I avoid such a fate. You must teach me, Bo Tao."

He frowned. "You already know more than any other virgin about being a political wife. Your mother taught you well."

"But I know nothing about being a concubine," she said. "Nothing about pleasing the emperor."

He groaned and rubbed a hand over his face, at last understanding what she asked. "Yi Zhen is not an easy man to please."

She took a breath. "You said a man in lust will do many things."

"Of course—"

"If I had met you before coming to the Forbidden City, I could have tried for something different."

He almost laughed. He had spent nearly all his moments in the last few days thinking what if and what might have been. He knew exactly how useless those fantasies were.

"But I am here," she continued. "And I must make the best of the life I have chosen. If I don't find a way to satisfy the emperor, then I am doomed to the lowest harem. I will be—"

"The lowest girl in the lowest harem." He had tried to warn her of such a fate before, but she hadn't listened. And now it was too late.

"What's done is done."

He nodded. "You are smart to think of now rather than what could have been." Much smarter than he.

"And so you must help me. Please do not doom me to what you showed me in the harem window."

This time he did laugh. All these virgins and their families with their bribes and their smiles, didn't they understand he had no control over who was selected? "There is nothing I can do, Ji Yue."

"Yes, there is," she said as she slowly lowered herself to her knees before him. He thought she was dropping into a kowtow, but she stopped with her legs folded beneath her and her upper body straight. "You can teach me. Show me how to pleasure a man."

His mouth went dry. But not his jade stalk, which tightened in joy. But he could not believe she was suggesting this. She was a virgin! "You want to…to do what you saw in the window?"

She nodded, her hand slowly stroking the bulge in his pants. "I do not know how to do it to a man." She lifted her eyes to his. "And if this is all we can have, then I want you to teach me."

"So you can do it to Yi Zhen." His voice was harsh, his bitterness sour in his mouth.

"You are my only hope," she said as she stroked him. His body throbbed with her caress, and his blood pounded so hard that it threatened to drown out his thoughts. Then she reached beneath his tunic and touched the skin on his belly. He grabbed her hand before her fingers reached to the tie there. "You go too far!"

"Isn't this what you suggested a moment ago? Isn't this what you wanted?"

It was, but not like this! Not so that she could seduce his best friend!

"If we had met before I was the emperor's virgin, if you had come to the door of my house instead of secreting yourself away in my palanquin, then I would have found a way to become your wife. I would have waited if you asked. I would have forced my mother's hand and accepted your suit somehow."

"But I did not," he said in misery.

"You did not." She twisted her hand from his then quickly thrust it into his pants to pull the tie apart. The fabric loosened immediately, slipping down until it caught on his engorged organ. "If ambition is all that I have left, Bo Tao, then I will hold on to it like the lifeline it is." She looked up and he saw how fiercely she had thought about this, how determined she was to make the best of her life as it was now.

He reached out and stroked her face. "You are already becoming hard, Ji Yue. Ambition does that."

Tears shimmered in her eyes. "I planned to have myself expelled yesterday," she said. "The bruises were at their worst then. I could have claimed an illness. I even walked to the examination room in search of the doctor."

"She must be summoned from her home in Peking," he said softly.

"The physician was not there, and you had forgotten me."

"Never!" he cried. "But you had made your choice."

"No," she said. "My mother made my choice for me. She will not allow me back home. And you had forgotten me."

How those words cut him.

"And so my choice was to leave the Forbidden City to walk the streets—"

"I would not have allowed that."

She arched her brow. "Perhaps, perhaps not. You do not have the money or the political stability to support a discarded virgin."

True enough. He had to stay in the emperor's good graces or starve.

"In any event, I did not know what you thought. So I chose."

"To become a whore?"

She hissed in anger. "To *not* become a whore. To learn what it means to seduce an emperor." With a quick jerk, she pulled his pants down to his knees. "I do not even know what a man looks like, and I have less than two days to learn all I can about it." She reached up and boldly cupped his sack. He nearly cried out at the force of her grip. "Do you teach me then, Bo Tao?"

With his balls in her hand, he had no choice. He reached down and touched her wrist. "Gentler, Ji Yue, they are not ink stones."

She softened her grip, then she rolled him slightly in her fingers. "They seem so hard. Underneath."

His entire body trembled and it was a moment before he could breathe. "There is a point behind the balls that has special sensitivity."

"Really?" She tilted her head to look.

"Not yet!" he gasped. "Not yet," he repeated as his breath steadied into shortened pants. "Begin with the stalk then proceed higher," he instructed.

She did as he bid. He had to shed his tunic or else the sweat would stain it. Then he stepped away from her to remove all his clothing. If she wanted to see a man, then so be it. She would see all of him.

"Oh," she breathed softly as she looked at him from head to toe. "Is the emperor this muscled?" she asked.

"No," Bo Tao said with a touch of arrogance. "Though he takes special pride in his legs."

She nodded, obviously making a mental note. Then she stroked his legs, running her hands through the dusting of hair on his thighs, then up to the thicker part between.

"You are beautiful," she said. "I have seen coolies, of course. I watched them most closely when Mama wasn't looking. You are not so thick as them." She flashed him a smile. "I like your leanness better. Can I touch it now?"

Her words and her touch were like opium smoke; his thoughts floated away into sensation. He instructed her as best he could. She cupped and she caressed. She gripped his stalk and rolled her thumb over the head. And when she extended her tongue to taste, his buttocks thrust of their own accord. He breached the confines of her mouth.

She drew back in alarm, but he had to steady himself on her shoulders. "You are losing control," she said in awe. "I have made you lose control."

"Not yet, you haven't," he growled.

"Then I shall have to try harder." And she engulfed him in her mouth.

She won. As she swirled her tongue around him, he began to move. His hands burrowed through her hair and he thrust, thinking she would gag on him. She did not. She took him all and sucked when he pulled back. The fire roared through his blood and ripped through his mind. He erupted with the force of days of hardened frustration. And when he spilled, she drank. She sucked him, caressed him, and made him think he was in the most blessed heavenly realm.

Until he collapsed onto his knees before her. He fell, gasping for breath. And when his vision steadied, he saw her licking her lips. "Thank you," she said most solemnly. "Do we have time for me to practice again?"

He could not believe it. He did not think that such a woman could exist in the whole world, much less be here looking at him with such an earnest expression. It nearly killed him to think that she could never be his.

"Not yet, Ji Yue," he murmured. "Remember, you have yet to be punished. I have to make you scream."

Her brow contracted in thought. "Can it be done at the same time?"

He smiled. "Oh, yes."

"Then I wish to learn that."

He nodded, already gathering his strength. He would have one afternoon with this amazing woman. One afternoon that would have to last his entire life, and so he decided to enjoy it to the fullest. "Very well," he said, "but you must remember to scream. As if in pain."

She nodded most solemnly. "I will remember."

"Then I will teach you."

13

"YOU MUST UNDRESS," he said.

Ji Yue recoiled in shock, her heart beating triple fast. It was one thing to be the woman caressing him, bringing him to a place where he had no control over his body. It was quite another to remove attire that kept her safe. Except, of course, no cloth could keep her safe. The very idea was ridiculous, but she felt its protection nonetheless.

"If you wish to know how to seduce a man," he said softly. "It begins with your body."

"You will see my bruises."

"Your body will always be beautiful to me," he said. She saw honesty in his eyes, and her heart broke. How had she come to this?

But if her future was in a harem, many women to one man—or even no man when the emperor died—she would take what memories she could. So she put her hands on her buttons and began to pull off her clothes.

"No. Not like you are at a dressmaker's," he said. "Slowly. Shyly. But with a hunger in your eyes."

As a virgin, she should not know what he meant, but she felt an aching longing and a building excitement in what she did. And in what they risked together. She looked at him and let her thoughts pour into her face. She let him see her desire, her fears, and her desperate wish…

"My heaven…" he murmured. And if she doubted the desire in his voice, all she had to do was look down. His jade stem had stiffened again.

With shaking hands, he pulled the cushions from the couch behind her and laid them on the floor. There was little space in this tiny corner of a lesser palace, but from what she understood of the Forbidden City, he must be valued indeed if he had a room of papers and books all for himself.

She smiled at the thought that one day he might have a whole palace of his own—a home and a library with emissaries from Peking coming and going. And in that wonderful fantasy, she was pulling off her blouse and undershirt for her husband.

"Mama said that men love breasts," she told him as she looked down at her chest. "Is that true?"

He nodded then gestured to her. "Come lie down, Ji Yue. I will show you what men do with breasts they like."

She lowered herself to her knees. She had not yet pulled off her skirt, so he did it for her, unwrapping it as one would a jade statue: slowly and with great care.

He frowned as he tossed the fabric onto a stack of scrolls. "I do not like it that they hurt you and I did not stop it." He ran his hand slowly down her hip, touching the scratches and discolored bruises.

"Stop them when I am about to be killed," she said. "Anything less, and I must endure. Or fight back." She leaned forward to whisper in his ear. "Ask the doctor when she next comes. Ask her how many girls have bruises worse than mine."

He pressed his lips to her neck and swirled his tongue over a scratch there. "Brave warrior. How does the rest of you feel?" His hand brushed over her lower hair.

She gasped in response, her hips undulating without her willing it.

"You need no cream, you know," he said softly. "Your scent is sweet enough." Then he lowered himself over her body until he pressed his face to her thighs. "I could get drunk on such a scent."

She ached for him to touch her. She well remembered what he had done before, but this was too new for her to know how to ask for what she wanted.

"Do you want me to touch you here?" he murmured as his fingers toyed with her hair. He looked up and she saw a flash of hardness in his eyes. "I will tell you a secret, Ji Yue. The emperor will quickly have his fill of shy virgins. It is the bold, the mischievous and the unusual girls who will entrance him."

She nodded and found a bravery she only had with him. "Very well, then," she said firmly. "I want you to touch me like you did before. Between my legs."

He grinned. "No."

Her eyebrows rose in shock. "But—"

"You have already learned that. Today, I will teach you something different." And so saying, he pushed her down until she lay prone on the floor, her head pillowed by the cushions. He kneeled beside her hip. "I do not kiss your lips this time. Not with your makeup still on your face. Kissed lips are too easily seen."

She nodded. She had forgotten about the white face paint she wore for her dance.

"There is much that a man likes to do with breasts," he said as he idly lifted and shaped hers. His stroke alternated between firm and gentle, between light tugs and harsher squeezes of her nipples. And every caress was like breath to a flame, making her own breath shorten and her pulse pound. She squirmed from the torment he built inside her. "This is what I like," he said. "I like to watch how my touch affects you. I like to see your body shudder and your lips darken. But my favorite is when you gasp."

He accompanied his words with a sharp pinch and she whimpered in delight.

"That sound is nice, too," he said. But then he stopped short as footsteps and two men's voice sounded in the corridor.

She looked at their naked bodies and then up at the blocked doorway. There was no way she could dress fast enough before someone tried to open the door. And still his hands toyed with her breasts. She smiled at him, then put strength in her voice.

"No, master! I have done nothing!"

He looked at her, an apology in his eyes. "Bitch! Whore!" he bellowed. Then he slapped her bottom with the flat of his hand. The sound was loud, the sting very real, and she cried out in genuine surprise. He immediately soothed her flesh with his mouth, kissing at the red marks, but it was a very pointed reminder of the dangers she faced. If they were caught, she would be out on the street or dead.

Then before she could think further he hauled her one leg up. Again, the movement was abrupt, the invasion startling. "Oh, no, master!" she cried. "No!"

"Silence, whore!" he growled, then his fingers began to open her up. His touch made her belly spasm and she whimpered.

"Oh, no! Please forgive me!"

He leaned sideways, and his hair caressed her inner thigh as he pressed his mouth to her flesh. Her leg rose higher to give him better access.

"Aie!" she cried out in stunned shock at what he did, but oh, it felt so wonderful! His tongue burrowed and coiled. He pressed his lips flat against her body there, and while she shuddered and whimpered, he began to suckle.

"Painful cries, Ji Yue. You must sound like you're in pain." Then he straightened his legs so that he lay on his side. As she watched, he lifted one hand and slapped it hard on his own thigh. The sound echoed in the tiny room. "Scream!" he whispered. Then he did it again, only this time as his hand descended, his mouth pulled hard on her most sensitive spot.

"Aie!" she screamed. "Aie!" she cried again as he repeated the action. Over and over he slapped and kissed—one hard sharp pull then a pause that lasted too long. Soon she was sobbing for real, but not in pain.

Her wriggling brought her more in alignment with his body—only reversed. His organ was before her face, thick and dark red. She smelled his musk and knew that she wanted to taste him again. She meant to touch him slowly—gently—but what he did to her made her hands unsteady and her body wild. She must have gripped him too hard because he gasped, his hold on her thighs tightening almost painfully hard. That gave her the breath—and the boldness—to do what she wanted. She touched him lightly with her teeth, abrading around the head and rim.

He shuddered. "How did you learn that?"

She pulled away. "Is it good?"

"Everything with you is good," he said. Then he returned to stroke with his tongue. Long slow pulls from back to front, then a swirl and a push at the peak where her tremors began. He repeated the caress over and over as she mirrored his movements.

It was exquisite! Whenever her thighs tightened or her breath grew too short, he changed his tempo. He stroked slower, fuller, longer as she tried to hold on to the sensations. And as he worked on her, she tried to drink him. His hips seemed to move of their own accord, and he thrust large and thick into her. But then the sensations became too much. She arched her body against his mouth. She demanded more from him just as he pushed harder and hotter into her mouth.

Then he pressed his lips to that place. He flattened his mouth around it and began to suck, then stroke, then suck again with no space between each movement. She mimicked him—sucking, then swirling, then—

She erupted, her body convulsing in expanding waves.

She would have screamed, but he pushed deep into her throat. Her cry became a gurgle and she was grateful. Then she had no thought as waves of delight shimmered endlessly through her.

If only they could truly last forever…

If only she and Bo Tao could…

If…

She slipped back to Earth. They had rolled apart, falling onto their backs so they had enough space to look down into each other's eyes. She saw dazed joy shimmering in his.

Is this love? she wondered. Was this feeling inside simply her body's awakening as a woman? Or was it love? Could she feel this way with the emperor? Or did it center on Bo Tao alone? She didn't know, and that unsettled her even more. So she eased back onto her side and focused on Bo Tao. Only him. And she felt joy because the strain around his eyes had smoothed.

There were noises in the hallway: footsteps, eunuch voices. She released a whimper for their benefit, making a mental note to put on her clothing so that she looked like she'd been beaten. Then she turned back to Bo Tao. She pressed a kiss into his belly, loving the way his muscles rippled in reaction.

This was love. She was in love with Bo Tao. She'd wanted to hide from the realization, but it had come, anyway. She was in love with the emperor's best friend. She was in love with a man that she would see often, perhaps daily in the Forbid-den City, but she would be married to someone else.

She turned away, not needing to force the tears that streamed down her face.

14

Ji Yue MADE IT BACK to her room. Her legs were unsteady, her makeup was streaked with tears, and her hair was askew. To anyone seeing her, she was the picture of a beaten woman. To herself, she was a woman in love.

What a disaster! She did not join the virgins at dinner. Instead, she went and bathed in solitude. She said nothing to anyone, but of course, she was never alone. Even in the bathing chamber, a eunuch watched her. And so she was not surprised when the head eunuch came to her chamber that night. He would want to know exactly what had happened to her with Bo Tao. She barely looked at him until she realized there was another person stepping into her room behind the eunuch.

"Dowager Consort!" she cried as she dropped to the floor in a hurried kowtow. Ji Yue pressed her forehead to the ground, acutely aware that her hair was askew and her clothing loose. She glanced quickly at her smirking roommate Hua Si. That's why the damned girl hadn't undressed even though it was late. She'd known the dowager consort was coming!

Meanwhile, Ji Yue spoke to the floor. "My gravest apologies. I had no idea you were coming or I would have remained presentable."

"Nonsense, nonsense," the older woman said. "You may rise."

Ji Yue did, though she moved slowly, partly out of wariness, partly because she was so very sore. The dowager consort took a seat on her bed. She sat there stiffly, watching Ji Yue with narrowed eyes. Ji Yue did not make the mistake of sitting. Instead, she rose wearily to her feet to stand like a eunuch before the older woman, head bowed and hands clasped in front.

"How may I serve you, my lady?" she asked.

"Oh, my dear, I just came to see if you were hurt. After Sun Bo Tao's display this afternoon, I have been greatly concerned about your health."

It was not hard to bring up tears at the reference to Bo Tao. She had not thought loving a man would hurt so much.

The dowager consort leaned forward. "Did he beat you very badly?"

Ji Yue glanced nervously at Hua Si, who stood beside her, and then at the head eunuch, who loitered just as near. Did the dowager really think she would confess anything with those two in the room?

The woman understood, of course. The dowager clapped her hands. "Out! Both of you! I wish to speak to Virgin Ji Yue alone!"

The two clearly didn't want to go, but they knew their place. They prostrated themselves multiple times, but then scurried backward out of the room. Probably to press their ears against the wall. It didn't really matter. Ji Yue didn't intend to tell the dowager anything that couldn't be known by the whole of China. Or that's what she thought until she heard the lady's next words.

"So many changes," the dowager murmured. "It is hard and confusing for me. I cannot imagine how difficult it is for you girls." She smiled and looked kindly at Ji Yue. "I have heard of your mother. She's very smart. Do you miss her guidance?"

To her horror, Ji Yue's eyes teared up again. She couldn't speak, so she nodded in silent misery. Everything had been so clear when her mother was around. Her course had been obvious, her duties clear. And if she'd chafed at the restraints, at least she'd had no doubt about what she was doing. But now, out from under her mother's gimlet eye? She had nothing but questions and doubts.

"Tell me about your mother. Would I enjoy her company, do you think?"

Ji Yue swallowed her emotions away and forced herself to answer as demurely as possible. "I cannot presume to suggest who you would find enjoyable, my lady. I can only say that I miss her deeply. She always sees things more clearly than I."

The dowager pursed her lips in distaste. "That was a dull answer. I thought you understood that court life requires intelligence. You certainly can't survive on your looks." She wrinkled her nose. "Your feet are horrifyingly big. Therefore, your value to me is your mind."

Ji Yue lifted her head, startled to hear her mother's words so closely echoed by the dowager consort. "What do you wish me to tell you?" she answered.

"What did Sun Bo Tao do to you today?"

She swallowed and looked away. "He beat me."

"Do you know why?"

Ji Yue nodded then gave the answer the woman expected. "Because he lusts after me but cannot have me."

"And do you return that lust?"

Now there was a tricky question. Ji Yue took a moment to reason out her response. Everyone in the Forbidden City relied on spies. So to become useful to the dowager, all Ji Yue had to do was offer to become one of her spies. "I pretend to lust for him," she answered with a sly tone.

The dowager's charcoal-painted eyebrows rose in surprise. "Very wise of you. The lust is not real?"

Ji Yue shrugged. "He is a friend to your son. I can survive a beating if it means we women have a better understanding of the influences upon the great leader of our people." There, she had just shown the dowager that she was smart enough to be a spy. Now she had to convince the woman that she was no threat. But how?

She glanced to Hua Si's side of the room, and the idea came to her. Oh, it was so easy! She just had to convince the dowager that she could be controlled. She had to show the dowager that something very simple would keep Ji Yue completely in her grip.

So she looked down at her hands, her expression vulnerable. "Can I tell you a secret, my lady?" Ji Yue whispered.

The dowager quickly leaned forward. "Of course, my dear!"

"The poets talk about love. Sun Bo Tao is consumed by lust. I fear I am an alien creature because none of those things draw me." Ji Yue bit her lip as if she were betraying a great deficit. "There is only one thing that I crave."

"Really?" The empress was at the edge of her seat. "What is it?"

Ji Yue chewed on a fingernail and tried to look guilty. "My parents don't have a lot of money. I have two brothers who want to take the exam, but tutors are very expensive. And Mama says that the boys are our future."

"Quite right, quite right," the dowager said. "So you wish money for your brothers?"

Ji Yue blinked just like an ox. "Er, yes. Of course."

The dowager smiled and patted her hand. "What a noble goal, Ji Yue, but that is not really the truth, is it?"

Ji Yue hunched her shoulders and shook her head. "Um, no. Not really."

"So what do you want?"

"Um…" She kept her voice low in case Hua Si was indeed listening through the walls. "Do you like candied leechee nuts?"

She frowned. "Candied fruit?"

"Have you ever tasted honey? I did once. My father had it." She closed her eyes in pretend rapture. "It was the most amazing thing I have ever tasted."

"You like sweets?"

Ji Yue felt a blush heat her face. It was shame because this had to be the biggest lie she had ever told. "Would you like to see?" She pulled the dowager consort over to a space behind Hua Si's trunk, then she pulled out a cache of candied sweets.

"But that is Gao Hua Si's trunk."

Ji Yue giggled. "I know. I put it there so people would think it is hers."

Meanwhile the dowager frowned as she leaned back and looked hard at Ji Yue. "You want sweets. That's it?" She didn't sound as if she believed it.

Ji Yue quickly replaced the stash after stealing a couple of pieces. Then she looked at the dowager with calm, honest eyes. "You are right that I am smart. A smart woman understands what she wants and how to get it. Do I want to carry the emperor's son? Of course. Do I know that there are spies and manipulations everywhere in the Forbidden City? Of course. And if I wished to hold the reins of influence, then someone might indeed fear me. But…" She shook her head, and her expression turned genuinely sad.

"But?" the dowager prompted.

Ji Yue thought of Bo Tao, of the things they had shared and done together. The tears that flooded her eyes were genuine.

"But I am working to manipulate one man and already it has cost me. I do not wish to do more." She abruptly leaned forward, wincing as if in great pain. "My lady, I will do whatever you ask. I will use my intelligence to watch and report whatever you want. The only thing I ask is that I become one of your pampered pets—the girls who are always at your side during meals. That I never go without food ever again!"

The dowager pursed her lips. "For a girl who is so hungry, you have missed many meals."

Ji Yue nodded. "Mama said I must. She often denied me at home because she said I would get fat."

The dowager studied Ji Yue's figure critically. "Fat women squeeze their babies."

"I know!" Ji Yue snapped. Was she really that fat that people could so easily believe this lie? "My lady, I am smart enough to know my weaknesses and my desires. I could be a great aid to you."

"Humph," was the woman's only response. She wasn't convinced, but she wasn't unconvinced, either. Ji Yue allowed her gaze to drift back to the secret cache. The candy had been delicious and she had missed dinner. Her mouth was watering for more.

"Go on," the dowager said softly. "Take another. I don't mind."

"Do you…do you want one?" she asked.

"No, no, dear. You go on."

Ji Yue flashed a grateful smile then dashed over to the candy. With her one stolen taste of food, her stomach was cramping in hunger. It was all she could do not to finish Hua Si's entire hoard.

"Careful," the dowager admonished. "There will be nothing left for tomorrow."

Ji Yue reluctantly put back what she had in her hand, then returned the whole cache to its hiding place. "Oh. Of course."

The dowager nodded then pushed to her feet. "Good night, Ji Yue."

Ji Yue had her mouth full and could only scramble to her feet. She didn't dare speak. With a distracted air, the dowager consort waved casually and glided out. Ji Yue barely had time to scramble back to her bed before Hua Si came bursting in.

"What happened? What did she say?"

Ji Yue shrugged, too tired to play games anymore this day. All the deception, all the court politics were giving her a bad headache. So she simply twisted her hair into her sleeping braid and climbed into bed. Behind her, Hua Si huffed in disgust and began to undress. Ji Yue closed her eyes and tried to sleep, but her thoughts would not stop whirling in her mind.

Was this what her life would be like from now on? Would she spend her days pandering to the dowager consort and her nights praying that a child took root in her belly? She winced at the idea of letting the emperor touch her as Bo Tao had. But what would happen to her if he did not choose her? Would she really end up like the concubines in the window? Of course not, she realized. She didn't lust after another woman's touch or even the emperor's caress. She wanted Bo Tao. No one else would do for her now.

How could she have been so stupid? How could she have fallen in love? And with the emperor's best friend? She curled onto her side and cried for real.

SHE WAS WOKEN hours later by a soft finger poking insistently into her side.

"Virgin!" It was a man's high voice. "Virgin Chen Ji Yue, you must wake."

She blinked, then groaned as she rolled over. How could an afternoon of such pleasure create so many aches now?

"Virgin Chen Ji Yue is called."

She blinked in the darkness and finally made out the moon face of a eunuch she'd never met before. "Called where? By whom?"

The man lowered his voice to a dark whisper. "The master of the festival calls you." Then when she didn't answer, he frowned at her. "Sun Bo Tao."

"I know who the master is," she snapped, irritated not by the interruption but by the sudden tightening in her throat, the leap of her heart in her chest and the rapid moistening in her womb. How would she ever be the emperor's wife if the mere mention of another man's name set her entire body tingling?

"You must come now!" he ordered.

It took everything in her to resist the eunuch's command. She didn't know if Bo Tao had truly sent the summons. It seemed an extremely risky way to call her, though he had used eunuchs before. If this was a fake summons, then she was being led into a trap. No virgin could be caught sneaking out at night to meet a man, even if he was the master of the festival. Especially if he was the master of the festival, since he was the one *whole* man in all of the Forbidden City.

But what if the summons were real? What if Bo Tao needed her? It didn't seem likely, but the fear in her heart burned like truth.

"No," she rasped, though the word hurt like a knife. "No, I cannot be beaten again." She rolled back onto her side and clutched her knees tight to her chest. It was the only way she could keep herself from changing her mind.

"He will be very angry!"

"Then he will beat me again tomorrow. Not tonight."

She waited in tense silence, wondering if the eunuch would bodily drag her from her bed. She half prayed that he would.

But after a hundred heartbeats, she heard him sigh and shuffle away. That left Ji Yue to spend the rest of the night in anxious fear. Who had sent the eunuch? Could it truly have been Bo Tao? What would he think? And if it wasn't Bo Tao, then who was testing her?

The questions didn't ease until dawn began to lighten the sky. By then her mind was so exhausted that it sputtered into silent fantasies. As she watched the dawn lightening the sky, she pretended Bo Tao lay beside her, tucking her safely in his arms. She imagined the heat of his body, the brush of his breath in her hair and his organ thick and hard inside her. What would she have to give up to have that for real? she wondered. What could she do to make her fantasies come true?

Nothing, she decided. Nothing could make them come true no matter how much she prayed.

15

BO TAO WAS IN TROUBLE. Everybody knew he had spent the afternoon with Ji Yue. And everybody was speculating on whether he'd beaten her or had sex with her. He'd tried to hide away from their speculation. He wasn't at all sure he could fake the angry contempt that would lead a man to beat a woman. Better to hide in his office and work on the things he should have been doing that afternoon.

He succeeded for a time. But when his best friend the emperor sauntered into the room around midnight, Bo Tao knew he was in trouble. If anyone could catch him in a lie, it would be Yi Zhen.

"I am not pleased with you," said the emperor.

This was bad. Yi Zhen was clearly in a mood to toy with him. Bo Tao's best bet was to play for time. So he took a very long moment to finish his last calculation, make his notation, then set aside his abacus with a sigh. The final touch? He rubbed his eyes. Only then did he look at his emperor. "What? And by the way, your eunuchs are robbing you blind."

"Hmm."

Bo Tao cringed internally. The eunuchs were usually the best way to distract Yi Zhen. He and Bo Tao had spent many long hours debating tradition versus cruelty. At the moment, the centuries-old castration practice remained, but Yi Zhen was thinking about making some very bold changes. Unfortunately, that was not on his mind today.

"I am very displeased with you," the emperor repeated.

Bo Tao kept his face as blank as possible. "Why?"

Yi Zhen stepped fully into the room, but he didn't sit. "Did you sleep with her?"

Bo Tao's eyes never wavered. "No." He'd never confess how close he came to taking her, though. Or how many times.

"You didn't beat her. You don't even beat eunuchs."

Bo Tao considered lying, but he knew he'd never get away with it. Instead, he let his gaze slide to the slivers of broken ivory in the corner. He'd smashed the ugly statue within seconds of her departure this afternoon.

"I humiliated her," he said with absolute truth.

"You can kill a Dutch envoy without blinking, but one virgin makes you smash a carving of an Immortal."

Bo Tao frowned. "I thought it was a badly done penis."

"Hmm." The silence stretched on until Bo Tao was nearly screaming. Then Yi Zhen abruptly folded his arms across his chest and thrust out his chin. "I could have you killed for playing with one of my virgins."

"You could have me killed for pissing in a pot. You're the Son of Heaven."

"She's *my* virgin."

"I know that."

"You're supposed to be figuring out which one would be best as an empress."

"She qualifies."

Yi Zhen was quiet again as he stared across the desk at his friend. The man still hadn't sat down, but towered above like the near-god he was supposed to be. "She spurned you, didn't she?"

Bo Tao clenched his jaw, the truth hovering on his tongue.

No, he could say. No, she wants me as much as I want her. Then maybe his best friend would relent. Maybe Yi Zhen would give up one of his precious virgins to his childhood companion. Or maybe he would kill them both. With Yi Zhen, he never knew.

"I wanted to force her."

"You've never raped before."

Bo Tao shrugged. He was doing a lot of things he'd never done before.

"I could give her to you," Yi Zhen said.

Bo Tao's head snapped up, and his eyes narrowed almost to slits. What game was his friend playing?

"Would you like that?" Yi Zhen pressed.

"Yes."

Yi Zhen smiled, and for a brief moment, Bo Tao allowed himself to hope. For one wonderful, amazing moment. And then his hope was crushed.

"I could, but then we would never know."

Bo Tao's hands tightened into fists on the desk. He didn't bother to hide them. "Know what, *Emperor Xian Feng?*" He pushed to his feet, fury radiating out of him. "What do you want to know? How else may I serve the Dragon Throne? Do you want my blood? My spirit? What more do you want from me?"

Yi Zhen's smile grew cold. He liked that he had pushed Bo Tao to a show of temper. "I want to know if she would rather have me or you."

Fury boiled through Bo Tao. He slammed his fists onto the desk and leaned forward. "She is not a toy in a child's game! Marry her, fuck her, sire a whole damned nation out of her!" he screamed. "But do not play games like this with her. She deserves better!"

Yi Zhen raised his eyebrows, obviously enjoying Bo Tao's

fit of temper. It was the same damn game they'd played as boys. No matter what Bo Tao did, whether he was faster, smarter or even crueler than his friend, Yi Zhen always had the upper hand. Yi Zhen was the emperor's son, and Bo Tao was not. In the end, all was given to Yi Zhen. Always.

And now the emperor relaxed. His smile remained as cold as ever, but now he dropped onto the couch. It was the very couch that Ji Yue had laid her clothing upon, the very couch where she had sprawled naked. And now it was the emperor there, sitting with a triumphant look in his eyes.

Bo Tao groaned, his spirit squirming in torment. "Yi Zhen, what do you want from me?"

"If she is a virgin on our wedding night, then you will get whatever appointment you desire. Name your position. Name your salary."

Bo Tao nearly sobbed. "How many times have you promised me that?"

The emperor shrugged. "This time it is true. I have written it down." He tossed a sealed scroll onto Bo Tao's desk. "Whatever you want, you shall have it at whatever salary you require. But only if she is a virgin on our wedding night."

Bo Tao's mouth went dry. His hands shook as he opened the scroll and saw his friend did not lie. "You intend to make her your empress?"

"Is she the best?"

He had to nod. It was the truth.

"Just make sure she screams *my* name when I fuck her." And with that, he pushed up from the couch and left.

BO TAO DID NOT SLEEP that night. He wandered through the dark and twisting passageways of the Forbidden City. He stared up at the home of the imperial virgins and fought the need to see her, to talk to her. He forced himself to walk away, then ended up in the tree platform watching another concubine "show." The very sight nauseated him, and yet he could not leave.

Was this what his future held? Staring at depraved shows, remembering stolen moments with the woman who would soon be empress? Ji Yue would never be seen through this window. She would be busy raising the next emperor and quietly helping to guide a nation.

He would have to leave. He knew he could not be anywhere near the empress without remembering, without thinking of how it felt to have her hand stroking him, her mouth surrounding him. He could not look at his couch without remembering her flushed skin as he brought her to fulfillment or how her body had writhed beneath his lips.

He would never be able to hide his thoughts from Yi Zhen. And though his emperor might be forgiving now, Yi Zhen was not known for his patience. He would not tolerate one of his closest advisors panting after his empress.

Bo Tao had to leave. He would pick a position far away from the Forbidden City, perhaps as ambassador to England or some other barbarian land. He would marry a political wife, someone who would not expect passion in her bed. Then he would sire a brood of children and think no more of Chen Ji Yue.

He dropped his head against the tree trunk and pushed the thought of her body from his mind. But that only reminded him that Ji Yue had other values. Her notes showed keen insight. If she were a man, he would hire her as his assistant and train her in the ways of politics. With the right guidance, she could become a fearsome leader and a great resource to the Dragon Throne.

But she was a woman, and her skills would make her the perfect empress. As a loyal bannerman, Bo Tao had sworn to give his life to the Dragon Throne. She was just one woman. Did his lust overrule his patriotism? Never! But what about love? Was love stronger than loyalty?

With a brutal curse, he left the concubines' display. He found himself once again staring up at the virgins' palace and praying that she would come out. Could he find a way to touch her again? Was there a way to risk a nightly dalliance? He toyed with the idea of overthrowing the entire government just so he could establish his own dynasty with her.

It was nearly dawn when he finally accepted that he was a fool. She was an empress-to-be, and he was *not* the emperor and never would be. If only she would come outside. He would hold her, and they could watch the dawn together. They would talk about unimportant things, and his spirit would quiet, his worries ease. If only…

He turned and left the Forbidden City. He was only torturing himself here. There was no hope for him and Ji Yue, and yet… As he walked through the gate from the Forbidden City into Peking proper, a kind of madness seized him. Looking out into the dark city, he knew that there was a world beyond the walls of the imperial city, beyond China itself. A whole world where he could carve a place for himself and Ji Yue. If only he dared. If only she dared.

But he had to be very careful. He didn't know if he was being trailed, if some spy somewhere would see him. He couldn't afford to take the risk. So with all semblance of despondency, he hailed a rickshaw to take him home. He entered as usual, climbed into bed as usual. Then, when he was sure any possible spy would believe he'd fallen asleep, he slipped out of bed, darkened his skin with dirt and donned coolie pants and hat. Though his body ached for rest, he crept from his own home and headed for the docks.

16

JI YUE DID NOT SEE BO TAO that day. She searched for him discreetly. She prayed that every time she turned a corner, he would be there waiting. But she had to appear as if she didn't want, didn't yearn for even the slightest view of him. The constant pretending was giving her a terrible headache, but she consoled herself that if she were caught, she could claim to be watching for the emperor instead. After all, that's what all the other virgins were doing.

They were less than two days away from the final selection. All the remaining virgins would be brides, but what level of bride was still to be determined. The only examination left was the last verification of virginity. Excitement was mounting, now that everyone knew they would end up in one harem or another. The virgins' days were occupied with etiquette instruction. Ji Yue was taught how an imperial consort sat (beautifully), how she should eat (sparingly), how she should walk (rarely and with great beauty) and what she should say (nothing). The head eunuch was in charge of this instruction, and Ji Yue did her best to fade into the background. Unfortunately, that only increased his tight-lipped criticism of all she did. Meals, of course, were the worst. The dowager's critical eye missed nothing. And if she did, someone else was sure to tattle. Ji Yue had never met so many gossiping, backstabbing women. She certainly had never expected to live her life among them!

Worse, Ji Yue had an extra layer of deception to maintain during meals. After all, she was supposed to have a secret, near undeniable craving for food and sweets. So she had to remember to eat her food almost furtively, her hand motions a little rushed. Her anxiety needed to be clear but under the surface. Which soon created a very real problem with her food. One minute she really was starving, and the next she couldn't even face it.

And still Bo Tao stayed away. By the end of the evening meal, Ji Yue had worked herself into a state of high anxiety. She was convinced he had sent the message last night, and that she had failed him. He was now lying dead in some Peking garbage heap because she'd spurned him. The idea was completely ridiculous, but that didn't stop her imagination from running wild. If a messenger came to her tonight, nothing would keep her from going.

Fortunately, the messenger came before the final undressing. A eunuch sidled up to her as she was brushing out her hair. Though many girls kept their hair glued up for practical reasons, Ji Yue had never liked the feel of it, like a heavy brick upon her head. So she took the extra time every day and night to brush it out. Tonight, a pair of soft male hands pulled the brush away from her. She glanced up in shock at the pale-faced eunuch who immediately began stroking her with a too-gentle touch.

"What are you doing?" she said as she tried to jerk her head away.

Underneath the brush, he grabbed a hunk of her hair and held her firm. Apparently, the eunuch was a lot stronger than he looked. She glared at him in the mirror and fought the urge to grimace. First she had to know what he wanted. But she didn't have to treat him nicely to find out.

"Do you know," she drawled, "that even a clean man—" that was the euphemism for a eunuch "—will feel great pain when hit hard in the groin. I understand some even pass out."

In the mirror the eunuch's eyes widened and he softened his grip on her hair. But he did not release her. "I bring you a message," he whispered. "You are to come with me to speak with the emperor."

So, not a message from Bo Tao. Her eyes stung more from that than the pain of having this man's meaty fist wrapped around her hair. She lifted her chin. "I do not believe the emperor would send someone as brutal as you. Release my hair now or suffer as only a man can."

He relaxed his grip, and she twisted her head away from him. Then she held out her hand for the brush. He gave it to her carefully, obviously afraid that she might beat him with it.

"You may leave now," she said.

He didn't move. Instead, he gestured out her window. "It is not just you, Virgin Chen Ji Yue. Others have been asked to a private audience."

She didn't want to look; she was certain this was a trick. And yet her gaze was drawn to the window nonetheless. Was Bo Tao out there waiting in the shadows? No. But she did see three virgins being escorted somewhere. Each was accompanied by a eunuch, but the girls did not seem to be struggling. If anything, they appeared excited. Unfortunately, she couldn't see well enough to know which of the virgins had been selected.

"Who goes to this special audience?"

"Are you scared?" he taunted. Then his gaze grew sly. "There will be food there. Special treats that are the emperor's favorite."

Definitely a trick, but now she was caught in her own lies. If she were indeed desperate for sweets, this would be just the lure to get her to comply. She had to reassure the dowager consort that she could be manipulated by food. She had to keep on the dowager's good side at least for two more days, until after the final selection. Which meant…

Which meant she was just making excuses for herself. She wanted to go, if only because she might see Bo Tao. It wasn't likely, but she would have no chance if she sat here brushing her hair.

"Chen Ji Yue!" the eunuch hissed. "You must come now or not at all!"

She pushed up from her chair. "I will come." He reached out to take her arm, but she jerked it away. "I will walk on my own." It was a false reassurance. The eunuch was clearly stronger than she was, but at least this way she could run if she had to.

The eunuch bowed to her, his manner vaguely condescending. He knew more than he was saying, but she could think of no way to get the information out of him. So she simply gestured him ahead. She would follow and keep a wary eye out for problems. And for Bo Tao.

They moved quickly through the Forbidden City. To her surprise, two more girls were being ushered ahead. And straight to the emperor's palace! It couldn't possibly be a real appointment with the emperor, could it? The prospect made her heart race. She would make a better impression this time. She wouldn't talk about insurgents or peasants or anything political at all. She would be sweet and beautiful and…

Oh no! Her hair was still down, flowing about her back like a washer girl's. "Wait!" she panted. "I must fix my hair."

"There isn't time," the eunuch replied. "Besides, he likes

it better this way. Do you think the timing is accidental? He wants you in partial dress."

Her hands hovered about her head in indecision. She didn't know what to believe or whom to trust. If only she could see Bo Tao. If only...

But he wasn't here, and she would have to do her best without him. Remembering the way Bo Tao loved touching her hair, how he'd stroked it and buried his face in it, she decided to leave it down. Bo Tao liked her hair free, perhaps the emperor would, too. And why, oh, why couldn't her heart beat fast at the thought of seeing the emperor rather than Bo Tao?

They made it to an entrance hidden by trees and a walled garden. She looked nervously at the opening. Once she stepped through that door, she would be trapped. But they were at the emperor's palace. She couldn't afford to waste this opportunity. And maybe Bo Tao lurked in a darkened room just inside. So with a last glance about her, she nodded her head and ducked inside.

"This way, virgin," a man's voice sneered.

She glanced behind her for the eunuch who had escorted her, but he had not followed her inside. The last she saw of him was his leering grin as he closed the door.

"This way," the voice repeated from deeper inside. She looked down the hallway and saw the head eunuch half illuminated by a lantern.

"This is really a meeting with the emperor?" she breathed, hurrying forward. The head eunuch would not be here otherwise, would he?

"The emperor will be watching," the man responded. "See that you perform as instructed."

She slowed her steps and pretended to play with her hair. This was clearly a trap of some kind. The eunuchs were acting too slyly, but how did she protect herself? "Perform how? What am I to do?"

"As you are instructed," he repeated. Then he stepped fully into the shadows such that the light fell upon a recessed door. "Inside there, virgin."

She couldn't go in blindly. Anything could be on the other side! So she started to take a step back. But just at that moment, another virgin was pushed into the hallway. It was Li Fei, the girl from the country who was the closest Ji Yue had to a friend among the virgins. Her eyes were huge in her pale face and a nervous giggle betrayed her anxiety.

"Ji Yue, have you been ordered to come, too? Well, of course you have. I mean he noticed you that very first night. You know, when we were celebrating the defeat of the Taiping. Of course, you didn't do so well then, but you're here now. Your hair is down. Are you sure you don't—"

"You are late!" snapped the head eunuch. "Hurry up! Inside now!" He grabbed hold of Li Fei and dragged her forward.

Ji Yue tried to stop them, but there was no room. The head eunuch shoved Li Fei, who in turn stumbled into Ji Yue and pushed her straight into a room hazy with a dirty, bluish smoke.

Li Fei immediately started coughing. Ji Yue's eyes watered, but she was more used to the smell of men's tobacco. Her father loved to smoke after dinner. Except this smell was more than just tobacco. It included opium, spiced teas and men. A lot of men.

"We should leave," Ji Yue murmured. "Now."

To her credit, Li Fei did not argue. She had stopped coughing, but her eyes were watering enough that the black makeup around them was smudged. Ji Yue backed up and felt for the door. She couldn't find it. She spun around, but all she could see was the flat panel of a painted wall. There was a latch somewhere. There had to be!

"Hey ho! Another one!" a man's voice called out in the coarse dialect of Canton.

Male cheers responded and suddenly someone grabbed hold of her arm. Ji Yue tried to jerk free, but he was large and strong, and when she looked up into his face, she saw he was a white man like those from the Dutch envoy.

She would have screamed, but her throat had closed off in terror. Beside her, Li Fei did better. She jerked back from her captor and screamed, "White devil!"

Crack! Li Fei's head snapped back as her captor backhanded her. This time a squeak of alarm managed its way out of Ji Yue's throat, but that was all the sound she made as her own captor lifted his arm threateningly. She braced for the blow, raising her arm to block it and adjusting her body to kick the brute right between his legs. She doubted this one was a eunuch. He would feel her blow for certain.

But a voice stopped her. "Do not be afraid, virgins," the man said in a high voice. It was Duan Xu, the head eunuch's favorite assistant. "The emperor wished you brought here to entertain our guests." He sauntered forward, a pipe in his hands. "Take a breath. It will help relax your fears."

"That's opium," Ji Yue guessed.

Duan Xu smiled. "Have you always wanted a taste? Have some. The emperor's special gift to you."

"No, it's not," she snapped. She scanned the room quickly, looking for a way to escape. She saw a dozen or more men—white and Chinese—all lounging throughout the room. The opium smokers were obvious by their glazed looks. Unfortunately, there were not many. The others drank or leered at the other virgins in the room. All of the girls had a pipe pressed to their lips.

And nowhere did she see an exit.

The white man grabbed the pipe and brought it to her face. He was saying something and smiling as if his doglike voice would reassure her. She fought him. She kicked and punched, but he was much too large and she was backed up against a wall with him on one side and a eunuch on the other. They pinned her head and pushed the pipe to her lips.

"Don't waste it!" he growled.

She couldn't move her head. Fortunately that helped her keep her lips sealed. She would not put that foul thing in her mouth! She would not!

Pain lanced through her belly. The eunuch had punched her! She gasped in shock, her knees crumpling beneath her. But the white man was there holding her up by her head. And sweet hot smoke filled her lungs.

No! But it was too late. She had breathed, and the sweet feel of it was...like duck feathers...soft down in her head and blood.

Then it was gone. She frowned as she took more deep breaths. She didn't want the opium smoke, and yet part of her already mourned its loss. Glancing to the side, she saw Li Fei in a similar state. Her skin was pale except for the angry red mark on her cheek. Her body was still held by her captor, but she was not fighting. In fact, her gaze followed the opium pipe as it was pulled away.

"No," Ji Yue said, trying to force an authority into her voice. "This is wrong. We are imperial virgins."

Someone responded, but she didn't understand his words. The other men did, though, and their laughter boomed in the room. Then she saw something that brought true fear to her heart. It was hard to see clearly through the smoke and the press of men. The eunuch dragged her forward, pulling her relentlessly, though she still tried to struggle. She was moving to a line of men. Were they pulling off their pants?

They were! All in a line, Chinese and white, their pants at their feet as they stood with organs proudly displayed. And like all boys, they laughed and mocked one another while each of the girls was dragged forward.

"What are you doing?" gasped one of the virgins. "I should not see this!"

At least Ji Yue was not the only girl who tried to protest. But not one of them was able to fight. All too soon, she and Li Fei joined the others in a line facing the men and their naked organs. She was pushed to her knees. Right before her eyes was a man—a white man with hairy legs and a terrible smell. His organ stuck out in front of her like a skinny, red slug. Compared with Bo Tao's penis, the man's seemed like a thin writing brush.

She fought the urge to vomit, but she was held fast by her hair. Damn her hair! She should never have left it loose.

"This is wrong!" she said again, appealing to the eunuch Duan Xu. "Why would you shame us so?"

If he heard her, he didn't acknowledge it. He was having too great a time laughing at the women. Ji Yue did not understand all the words, but she caught the meaning. They were judging the girls' bodies in the most crude manner.

"I will not—" she began, but was rapidly silenced by a hard jerk on her hair.

"She needs more opium!" her eunuch captor called in guttural Cantonese.

"No!" she snapped. "No, I won't!"

"Much more!" laughed a man with a pipe. Except he did not release his grip on it.

The white man leaned forward. "Do as you're told, virgin. Or we will choose another way to find our pleasure. And you won't be called a virgin any longer."

Ji Yue trembled. She did not doubt him for a second. They would rape her if she did not comply. But she also feared they would rape her even if she did agree. Her only hope was to delay as long as possible until the men passed out from their drink and smoke.

"I am going to vomit!" she cried.

She was rewarded with a another yank on her hair. "Do so and you will lie in it as I spread your legs. Do you understand?"

She nodded as she blinked back her tears. Meanwhile, the eunuch Duan Xu took his place at the end of the double line. "Virgins!" he called. "Listen, virgins! You are here because the emperor has assigned you a special test to verify your skill as a wife."

Ji Yue did not want to look at the man. She already knew what was coming. She had no wish to see the bastard's gloating face as he spouted lies.

"Do you know what a wife does, virgins? I will tell you. A wife brings satisfaction to her husband." One of the girls began to cry. Within seconds, the opium pipe was put to her lips. "Before you is a man's organ," continued Duan Xu. "The emperor wishes to see who can bring that man satisfaction first. The winner will gain a special prize! Begin."

No one moved. No one except the men who surrounded them. The eunuch used his grip on Ji Yue's hair to move her face forward. The man in front of her thrust his hips at her, pushing his wet tip into her nose. She reared back, but there was nowhere to go. She could tell from the sounds that the other virgins were being treated with equal brutality. So she did the only thing she could.

She reached up with both hands. She took hold of the horrible thing with all her strength, and she squeezed. She even used her nails.

The white man screamed and hit her about the head. She saw it coming and avoided the first of his wild blows, but the eunuch behind her still had a firm grip on her hair. The second blow caught her on the top of her head. That threw her far enough away that the white man was able to scramble backward, pulling his organ from her grip. But she had not released him and she felt her nails cut long scrapes off the narrow thing.

Meanwhile, she slammed her elbow backward into her captor. She connected with his upper thigh, and he grunted in pain but he did not release her. He threw her to the ground. Her shoulder and head landed painfully hard, but at least she was free. She tried to scramble away then, but she was too slow.

Someone grabbed her leg, twisting her painfully so that she landed on her back. She screamed and kicked, but someone else dropped hard onto her chest, pinning her to the ground. Rough hands grabbed her head and legs. And then another pipe was pressed to her lips.

17

A ROAR CUT ACROSS THE ROOM. Ji Yue thought it was the blood rushing through her ears or the echo of her own screams. The opium smoke was filtering into her blood, dulling her thoughts and her feelings. Sounds came from a distance with delayed meaning.

The man holding the pipe disappeared, and the pipe lay on the ground forgotten. Then she saw him: Bo Tao. His face was contorted in fury. He moved so fast—faster than any of the men—that he peeled her captor off her and threw him aside. She could breathe again, but she didn't move. She was watching her love. She could see every flex of his muscles, every bead of sweat on his face. His movements were fluid, the exchange of blows like the flow of water in an elaborate fountain dance, and yet she knew he gritted his teeth and she heard his grunt with every blow given or received.

She heard the screams of virgins, the bellows of other men, but Bo Tao consumed her vision and her thoughts. A part of her feared for him. Whenever someone else blocked him from her sight, she ached with the fear that he would not resurface, he would not survive. But he always did. He always came back to fight for her again.

Her heart swelled with love.

And then, to her delight, the room cleared. Bo Tao was free

to kneel down beside her, his eyes anxious with fear. Blood and sweat were smeared across his cheek, his chest heaved as he breathed in great gulps of air and his hand trembled as it extended to her face.

"Ji Yue! Ji Yue! Are you all right?"

"I love you," she said. She felt it so strongly that the thought and the words formed without pause. "I love you."

His body stiffened in reaction. His eyes widened and she watched him swallow, the corded bands of his neck standing out in stark relief. Then he pressed his fingers to her lips. "Shh, Ji Yue. You are not feeling well."

She wanted to say she was feeling quite fine, but she wouldn't argue with him. And it didn't matter anyway, because he wasn't looking at her. Though he kept one hand on her mouth, the other began pointing as he issued orders.

Ji Yue hadn't realized there were others in the room, others that had fought by Bo Tao's side. She had seen only him. Now she heard Bo Tao order arrests. The whites were to be escorted out of China, never to return. The other virgins were sent to a palace she hadn't heard of before—yet another building in the vast Forbidden City. And the doctor was sent for.

It wasn't until someone accidentally stepped on her hair that she realized she shouldn't be lying here on the floor. It was time she got her excruciatingly heavy body back to the safety of her bed. Except, of course, she wasn't thinking about her bed in the virgins' palace. There was no safety there. She wasn't dreaming of her bed back with her family in Peking. She could only think of Bo Tao's arms wrapped around her. How she wanted to rest her head on his shoulder and watch dawn soften the heavy, black night.

But that wasn't going to happen, she realized. She was an imperial virgin and would soon become an emperor's wife, even if she was locked in the lowest harem and never heard from again. Bo Tao was not part of her future, and she needed to remember that. She did remember that, but when she told herself to get up and go back to the virgins' palace, she remained curled on her side again with silent tears streaming down her face.

She heard a strangled moan above her from Bo Tao. She felt for his pain and wished for his sake that she could stop her tears. But she couldn't, so she buried her face into the dirty floor.

"You need to see the women's doctor!" he said harshly. Then she felt his hands gently gather her up. She wanted to say she could walk, but his arms felt so good as he pressed her tightly against his chest. Then she heard him say something else.

"Throw his body out for the dogs."

Someone had died? Curiosity and fear made her lift her head. Was it the man she had scraped with her nails? Could that kill him?

It was the eunuch Duan Xu. She stared at the body for a moment and tried to feel something. He had been a major instigator of tonight's terrible events, but he wasn't the sole one responsible. Still, she could not be sad that he was dead. In truth, she was grateful that she'd never have to face him again. Then another image filtered through her mind. She saw Duan Xu throw a heavy wood tray at Bo Tao's head. Bo Tao had ducked, spun and thrown a kick that caught the man under his chin. Duan Xu's head had snapped back and he had dropped as he lay now, his neck broken.

"You killed him," she murmured.

Bo Tao's arms tightened around her. "Does that bother you?"

She shook her head and buried her face against his chest. "Thank you."

Bo Tao uttered a very masculine grunt and then began walking. He carried her out of the emperor's palace. She closed her eyes, allowing the rhythm of his heart to mix with his steady stride. She felt the cool night air against her skin and the rippling pull of her unbound hair. She opened her eyes to see if the sky was lightening into dawn, but saw a thousand stars instead. It was deepest night, and she smiled. She would have more time to stay right here in his arms.

She closed her eyes and prayed that this moment would never end. She felt him step over the entrance to an inner courtyard and then again into another building. They maneuvered through passageways until he finally set her gently down on a pallet.

"Ji Yue, do you need a doctor right away?" he asked.

"No," she answered. "No, I'm fine. My head hurts, though."

He immediately began touching her head, probing her scalp with gentle fingertips. She winced once or twice, but mostly she liked the feel of his hands in her hair.

"Hmm," she murmured.

"I could kill them for what they did to you!"

She smiled. "At least I got to see you again. Where have you been?"

His expression sobered. "Did you mean what you said, Ji Yue? Did you mean it?"

She frowned. "What?"

"That you…" He had to clear his throat. "That you love me?"

She laughed. "Of course I did, silly. I do not let just anyone carry me across the Forbidden City. Come closer." Then she reached up and pulled him down onto the pallet with her, maneuvering back into his arms. "I like it here." She closed her eyes to appreciate his scent while his thumb stroked lightly across her cheek.

"We have some time before the doctor arrives. Do you want to sleep?"

"I want to watch the dawn with you," she said, her eyes still closed.

He didn't respond for a long time. He was quiet while she listened to the rapid beat of his heart.

"What would you give up, Ji Yue? What would you give to be with me like this always?"

"Everything," she said, burrowing her fingers under his shirt. She wanted to touch his naked chest.

"Would you leave the Forbidden City? Would you give up being empress?"

"We could live in a house near Canton. Our sons would play in the garden while we watch the ships come and go." She smiled at the lovely dream. "I would bear you many strong sons."

He lifted her chin and took her mouth in a fierce kiss. It was bold and powerful. The way his tongue swept through her sent tingles down her spine. And when he lifted his head, she smiled again.

"You would kiss me just like that every day."

"Every day and every night," he swore. His eyes looked fierce, his expression possessive. She liked the way he looked at her.

"Touch me, Sun Bo Tao. Touch me everywhere."

He hesitated, his hand stilling against her cheek. "You are not yourself, Ji Yue. They gave you opium."

She wanted to grab his face, she wanted to kiss him deeply. Instead, she brought his hand to her mouth. She held it to her lips and stroked her tongue across his palm.

"Ji Yue—"

Then she sucked one of his fingers deep into her mouth and heard him groan. She pulled his hand away and slid it down her body, forcing him to stroke her breast, her belly and her hip. And then she spread her legs as much as possible in her tight skirt and pressed his hand to her inner thigh. "I know my heart, Bo Tao." How she loved saying his name. "I love you. I want to be yours."

He kissed her then. She let her head fall back from his shoulder into the cradle of his arm. She let him thrust his tongue into her mouth while her breath quickened and her body trembled. And when his lips went from her mouth to her cheek then down her neck, she knew where he was going. She knew what he would do and she smiled.

"Yes, oh, yes."

He unbuttoned her blouse and pushed the sides away. He feasted on her breasts while lights danced behind her eyes and filtered into her blood. His beard brushed against her skin, and the lights trembled beneath her skin. He sucked on her nipple and her whole body shimmered.

She ran her hands through his hair, but it was held tight by his queue. Rising up onto her knees, she faced him, her legs spread wide. Then she reached around to unbind his hair. She wanted it undone, and yet she loved the silky feel of the long braid in her hand.

He turned his head, then tugged off the cord that bound his braid. "I will cut this from my head for you."

She laughed in delight at the ridiculous thought. The long braid was every man's sign of devotion to the Manchu emperor. It was mandated by law. Only the monks were allowed to shave their heads, and even they were held in suspicion because of it. She burrowed her fingers into his hair, spreading it wide as she went. "I like your hair."

He touched hers equally reverently. "I like yours, too."

She giggled. "Kiss me again."

He did. He plundered her mouth. Over and over he thrust his tongue into her, and the feel of it sent her wild with hunger. Her skirt was restricting her legs, so she lifted it up. She wanted his hands on her there, needed his mouth to do what they had done before in his office.

She reached for his member and found it quickly and easily. She stroked his thick, full length and knew that this was right. This was what a man felt like. He groaned in hunger at her caress and she thrilled at the dark vibration that traveled from his body into hers.

"Never has a woman done this to me," he said against her neck. His breath was hot as he shifted his hips. Her arms were between them, and she held his wet tip, rolling the moisture around and around with her thumb. But her other arm was free, and she let it flow around his hips and trim buttocks. What muscles he had! She squeezed playfully, laughing when his flesh barely moved.

He was looking at her, his expression fierce. She smiled at him, feeling her love swell for this serious, serious man. "I love how you feel," she said. Then she sobered. "I love how you look at me. No one has ever looked at me like that." How she wanted him. How she wanted to feel what other women felt, to just once have him where she most wanted.

"I want to marry you, Ji Yue. I want you to choose me."

"I do. I choose you." She rose up to kiss him. She wrapped her arms around his neck and plundered him as he had her. They were belly to belly, but she felt him between her legs. She knew where his organ was and…she sat. It wasn't a conscious decision so much as a need that compelled her. One moment she was above him, using her arms to support her weight as she kissed him deeply, completely and as fully as she knew how. The next moment she simply let her legs go weak. She dropped down, and he filled her in one beautiful, expansive, amazing moment.

He gasped, his eyes shooting wide. But the sound was just as quickly followed by a moan of both hunger and fear. "Ji Yue—"

She didn't want him to speak. She didn't want him to ruin this most wonderful moment. So she silenced him with another kiss, another exploratory, teasing, fabulous kiss. And as she did, she rose up on her knees just enough to feel him slide nearly out. She gave him a wicked, teasing smile and slid back down.

She saw him swallow and felt his arms tremble. "I love you," he said fiercely. "You are mine." The next time she rose up, he helped her. And then as she came back down, he matched her movement with a thrust.

He was inside her, thick and large. His face had gone rapturous and she thought how beautiful he looked. Then they began to move together. She controlled the ebb and flow of their movements. Though he helped, she decided what she wanted. When to lift, when to lower, how fast, how slow. And she found more joy in making his eyes flutter, causing him to groan or gasp, than she did in the feel of him hot and hard inside her.

Until she wanted more. Smooth slide. Hard pressure. He filled her again and her back arched in pleasure. But it was not enough.

He withdrew again, and this time she squeezed because he seemed to like it. Her hands tightened on his shoulders, and her knees gripped his hips. He thrust harder into her, and she laughed because it felt so right. She'd tilted her pelvis down to meet his movement, to feel the slam exactly where it was best. And when he rolled his hips against her, her breath caught on a gasp.

Their eyes locked together. She'd had no idea that this was possible. This wonderful tension—she'd felt it before. This build to ecstasy—she'd experienced it with him before. But the way their eyes locked, the total oneness with him—that was new. That was incredible.

They breathed together. They gasped together. And they built that quivering tension with perfect unity. He thrust and she soared. He withdrew and she shivered. Higher and higher. Until they touched...

Heaven!

"WE MUST GO," he whispered against her ear. "Sweet Ji Yue, I am sorry, but we must hurry."

She blinked. Shimmering delight still suffused her body—their bodies—since they were still joined. He gently raised her off him, and she moaned. She liked the way he cradled her in his arms. And she loved the fullness of him inside her. She noted regret in his eyes, but it did not stop him from gently setting her aside. With faster and faster motions, he pulled off his tunic and undergarment. Then his biceps bulged as he tore a strip from the cotton shirt.

"This was not the way to do it," he murmured. "I would have laid you in silk and covered you in perfumes." He glanced at her, the apology clear in his eyes. "But you are so beautiful, and you took me by surprise." He dropped a quick kiss on her lips. "I could not stop myself."

With tender movements, he used his torn strip to clean her lower body. And when he lifted the cloth away, she saw the dark stain of blood. Tilting her head, she peered closer. The lantern light was dim, but the truth was horribly clear.

"I—" she gasped "—I am..."

He quickly wadded up the cloth and made to throw it away.

But then he stopped and stared down at it. "I need to burn this," he said softly.

"I am not…" she said again, her mind replaying what she had done and said. What had she done? He had felt so wonderful, and she had been swept away on her own fantasy.

"I am sorry, my sweet, but we have to go. The doctor will be here soon."

Ji Yue pulled her legs together and curled her feet beneath her. What had they done?

He finished dressing, then he dropped to his knees before her. He held her hands and gazed into her face. She focused on him. She saw the dark center of his eyes and the loving curves of his cheeks. Even the length of his nose was beautiful.

"Listen to me, please. I have made reservations for us. There is a boat that will take us away at first light, but we cannot be caught here. Not now…" He glanced ruefully at the blood-stained cloth on the pallet. "I was so afraid for you, Ji Yue. I did not think, and then you were here, so willing in my arms. This was not smartly done, but—" he shrugged "—it is done. We must leave."

"I am no longer a virgin!" she cried. "I have shamed myself and my family!"

He stilled. She did not think he breathed. She didn't care. She was still reeling from what she only now began to understand.

"You planned this! You want us to run away from here! You planned all of this!"

He shook his head. "Not like this. Not now. I thought to talk to you." He frowned. "We did talk! You chose me!"

"I did," she whispered, but she hadn't thought clearly. "I wanted you. I love you! But…" A tear fell on her hand and she realized that she was crying. "My mother will commit suicide in shame!"

His face was pale, his jaw tense. "Ji Yue…" he began, but there were no words. Not now with her heart pounding and her mind reeling.

The thud of footsteps sounded outside. Bo Tao could do no more than stand, before the door was pushed open and the women's doctor stomped inside. Her gait was weary and her shoulders sagged, but her gaze was sharp as she looked from Bo Tao to Ji Yue and then to the wadded, bloody cloth. With a grimace, she spun and pushed the door shut. When she turned back to Bo Tao, her mouth was pressed into a thin tight line.

"It was not her fault," he said.

The doctor rolled her eyes. "In China, it is always the woman's fault." She grimaced. "And now she will be killed."

18

IT TOOK A MOMENT for Bo Tao to realize the doctor thought Ji Yue had been raped by a white devil. It was a reasonable guess. Many had seen Ji Yue on her back fighting those apes, and a surge of rage shot through him again at the memory.

"I came as quickly as I could," he said. "I spent the day in the city and didn't hear about the party until too late."

She bustled forward, coming to sit before Ji Yue, but her words remained for Bo Tao. "Nine virgins, Bo Tao. How could this happen?"

"Because the eunuchs are corrupt," he snapped. "I kill the Dutch who bring in bribes of opium, then not one day later Han Du Yu brings in a case to bribe the head eunuch. With the emperor away this night to dine with General Li, it was the perfect opportunity." How stupid he had been not to guess that something like this could happen!

"Can you prove it?" the physician asked.

He shook his head. "Not yet. I merely guess. But it does not matter, does it?" He rubbed a hand over his face, his gaze on Ji Yue. Was there a way to save her life? The punishment for the loss of virginity was death. It did not matter the cause or who was at fault, her honor was gone. She would have to commit suicide even if someone else pushed her neck into the noose that hung her.

The physician cursed under her breath. "How did you hear of it then? Duan Xu usually covers his tracks better."

Bo Tao had set a spy on Ji Yue, a eunuch he trusted to watch her every movement when he was not there. Unfortunately, the coward had been too afraid to interfere against the two most powerful eunuchs in the Forbidden City.

"It was well planned by more than just Duan Xu."

Ji Yue shifted, her words a near whisper. "The head eunuch was there. He pushed us through the secret door."

Bo Tao grimaced, his fears confirmed. "He and the dowager consort are thick as thieves. They likely chose the girls together. They picked the ones they wanted disgraced."

"Bitch," the doctor said under her breath. "There was no need to do such a thing."

Ji Yue abruptly pushed up on the pallet. Her gaze remained panicked, but at least her body seemed composed. "How are the other girls?"

"Hysterical," the doctor answered. "They all know their chances have been ruined." She glanced at Bo Tao. "And there will be much blame attached to you. You are master of the festival. He could order—"

"I know." Bo Tao could be killed for failing to protect the virgins under his care. "I should have been here. I should have watched things more closely."

The doctor sighed as she pushed Ji Yue gently back onto the bed. "Come, come. Let me see—"

"No," interrupted Bo Tao firmly. "You have examined her. She is like the others—high on opium, terrified, but not damaged."

The doctor stopped with her hand on Ji Yue's knee. "And if she is bleeding inside? Would you have her die in her sleep?"

That, at least, was one worry he could put to rest. "It was not that bad," he said softly.

The doctor's eyes narrowed on Bo Tao. She had known him from his youngest days. She had been at his birth and watched him run wild with Yi Zhen throughout the Forbidden City. She knew him, perhaps, even better than his own mother.

"She might escape death," she said softly. "Perhaps a mercy marriage to someone else might be allowed."

"No!" Ji Yue breathed. "The shame would be known by all. My father. My brothers!" She swallowed and gripped the woman's hands, drawing the doctor's attention back to her. "My family is…is not as wealthy as it might seem. A disgraced virgin would put an end to any work for my father as an imperial scholar." She shook her head. "My brothers' education, my mother's food, my father's livelihood—they all depend upon our connection to the Forbidden City. If I were to disgrace myself…" Her eyes shifted to Bo Tao. "There are other scholars anxious to take my father's place. Others who do not have my taint."

Her stricken expression was like a blow to Bo Tao's gut. "Ji Yue," he began, but she shook her head.

"My immorality will follow my whole family."

She wasn't referring to simply being thrown out of the Forbidden City. She was referring to his plan to run away, to escape and live with him in love.

Ji Yue looked down at her hands. "I cannot take my own happiness over the lives of my family. I simply cannot."

Her words were a death knell to his hopes and dreams. Then the doctor made it worse. "What if the emperor demands honor suicides from all of you?" she asked. "What good will that do when the eunuchs come with rope and tie your neck to a beam?"

Bo Tao saw the shudder course through Ji Yue's body. He took a step forward, wanting to soothe her fears, wanting to promise that nothing like that would happen to her. But he couldn't. In truth, the soldiers might even now be searching for him. His neck was by no means safe. After all, he was master of the festival, and he had allowed nine virgins to be ruined.

"Think, Ji Yue," he said to her. "Think of *all* the possibilities." He willed her to look into his eyes. He silently urged her to remember what he offered—a ship ready to take them away, an escape for the two of them. To his delight, she did lift her head, she did meet his gaze, and he believed she understood what he offered.

But in the end, she turned away. "My heart goes one way, and if it were only me, I would gladly follow it. But the moment I stepped inside the Forbidden City, I chose family over my happiness. I will not dishonor my family now." Her voice was dull, but he heard the steel beneath it. She would not hurt her family, which made her more honorable than him.

"Do you know what you risk?" His voice broke on the last word. Even if she escaped this disaster, even if she was allowed to remain without committing suicide, she had clearly made an enemy of the dowager consort and the head eunuch. Her life would be a misery. And his life would be a misery watching her. Heedless of the doctor beside him, he dropped to his knees before Ji Yue. "You would do this for your family's honor?"

"I do not blame you," she said. Then she stiffened her spine. "If something happens to me, will you see that my family has work?" He understood the unspoken message. If they were to run away together, there would be no one here to see that her family did not suffer any consequences.

"Of course, but—"

She looked at the doctor. "There are ways, are there not? To prevent pregnancy? And to fake virginity?"

The doctor grimaced. "It will be hard to fool the emperor. You will not be his first virgin."

She shrugged. "If it comes to that, I will already be his wife. It would shame him as much as me."

Bo Tao almost snorted. "Do not count on Yi Zhen thinking that way."

Her eyes met his. "But you will still be here to assure—"

"Yes, yes," he snapped. "I will look after your father. But you, Ji Yue…" He bit his lip. "Does your life mean nothing?"

She reached out and touched his cheek, the stroke so tender, so exquisite that he shuddered at the beauty of it. "A woman's life is to bring beauty and honor to her family and her husband. We have no honor or purpose beyond that. You know this as well as I do."

He knew. All the love stories in China ended with death. It was the only way to preserve honor. "You are smart, Ji Yue. Surely you can think of another way."

She shook her head. "I am an imperial virgin. Even in the lowest harem, I will bring honor and prosperity to my family. That was why I came to the Forbidden City in the first place." Her gaze sharpened on the doctor. "I am an imperial virgin, aren't I?"

The doctor sighed and glanced at Bo Tao. He gave a barely perceptible nod in confirmation. He would give the physician an excellent bribe for her part in faking Ji Yue's virginity.

"Yes," the doctor said with a crisp assurance. "But you should rest all day tomorrow to recover. As I have already examined you, you will not need to do so again with the other virgins." Then she glanced sharply at Bo Tao. "Provided, of course, that the emperor does not demand—"

"He will not. The only dishonor is on the traitors who created the party in the first place." He pushed to his feet. He

had to do what he could to mitigate the disaster and to be sure
that the blame fell where it belonged. "I must go." He looked
down with great regret at Ji Yue. "I will make sure that your
honor and your family's status are not harmed." He said it as
a vow and silently prayed that he could keep his promise.

Ji Yue nodded in gratitude.

"Stay and care for her, please," he said to the physician.
Then he looked one last time into Ji Yue's eyes. She had made
her choice, and he could not fault her for it. She had chosen
honor over love, her family over herself. With a bow of
greatest respect, he turned and left.

It was time to face an emperor's wrath.

19

THE TAINTED VIRGINS were quarantined, Bo Tao was disgraced and six eunuchs were whipped, two of them so badly that they were not expected to live. Ji Yue heard the news with the stoicism of an empty heart. The other girls in quarantine with her sobbed or had maidenly hysterics on a regular basis. During the noon meal, the head eunuch came and apologized for the grave mental illness of his subordinate who had perpetrated such a heinous crime. He told all of them that they would be allowed to return home to their families without disgrace.

No one left, of course. They all knew it was a lie. And no one dared say that it had been the head eunuch who had met them at the door to the palace and who had directed them inside. In such a way, the virgins hoped to buy favor with the evil man.

The dowager consort visited later that day. She went from room to room, a sly smile on her face as she praised their new quarters. It was to become the home for the lowest harem. She spent the most time in Ji Yue's bedroom. She complimented Ji Yue's bravery and confided that the man she had gripped was permanently maimed. Then she remarked on how wonderful it was that her son was so open-minded as to not require honor killings for them all. They would become wives despite everything!

Ji Yue did as was expected. She kissed the ground in thanks

for the emperor's generosity. Then she lifted her head and
pinned the dowager consort with a dark stare. She had not
been able to forget Bo Tao's comment that the dowager had
probably helped plan this disgrace. She didn't look away but
simply stared and wondered. And the longer she looked, the
darker the dowager's color became.

"I would have helped you, Dowager Consort," Ji Yue finally
said. "I would have seen to your comfort out of respect for
your place as his mother." She straightened up from the floor,
then made it to her feet. But the dowager did not let her leave.

"And what will you do now?" The question was half
taunt, half fear.

Ji Yue arched her brow and made her next words a vow. "I
will see that you get the honor and respect you deserve." Then
she walked away, knowing she had just declared the most
powerful woman in the Forbidden City as her enemy. It was
a foolish thing to do, and yet the petty vengeance felt right.
Worse, all sorts of possible slights and petty revenges came
easily to mind. In this way she soothed her own battered heart.

By evening she grew sick of her own thoughts. Revenges
she would never enact could not distract her for long from her
real pain, the ache of losing the love of her life. She could have
fled the country with Bo Tao. She could even now be lying in
his arms, dreaming of the sons that they would have.

If she had run, would her father really have been destroyed?
Would her mother truly have committed suicide from the shame?
It was a possibility, she knew, but would they have actually done
it? And if she was doomed to the lowest harem anyway, would
the emperor truly care if she escaped with his best friend? Would
he really punish two such insignificant beings when he had all
of China to oversee? Perhaps. Perhaps not.

She collapsed onto her knees before the fire, her eyes

watching the dance of the flames. She felt like the burning log, on fire and slowly turning into a tiny knot of black ash. Was she withering now after one day in disgrace? How would she survive after a year in the lowest harem? Or worse, how would she live after a year of running in terror from an angry emperor?

The choices collided in her heart and her mind. One moment she thought she would run to Bo Tao and beg him on her knees to take her from here. The next would have her crying for her mother and the shame that could destroy everything at home. And in that dark moment, she heard the one voice she most hoped and feared to hear.

"Virgins!" Bo Tao called. "The emperor has brought you a present."

She spun around, her heart leaping to her throat as she looked through her doorway. His expression was hard, as if frozen into place. She detected no softness in his eyes or his demeanor, and yet she thought his gaze lingered on her face. Did he see her tears and her regrets? She ducked her head in shame. She did not want to increase his suffering with her own. Head down, she slowly stood, leaving her room to join the other virgins in the main gathering place.

He watched her come into the center of the room. She knew it because her body tingled with awareness, but when she glanced up, his face was turned to the room at large. He looked over all the girls, his expression hard but his eyes sad. And then he held up nine red ribbons with a cheap monkey charm in the center.

"Virgins," he said again. "The emperor apologizes for the insult given to you last night. He gives you this token of his esteem and bids you wear it tomorrow during the final selection of his brides."

Silence greeted his words. All understood the meaning

behind the gesture. After all, the emperor could not remember which of the thirty-six remaining virgins were the ones who had been insulted by the white apes last night. But this necklace, this cheap monkey charm would identify them as clearly as a black, ugly smear across their faces.

Ji Yue winced at the unfairness of it all. But in the silence following Bo Tao's pronouncement, Ji Yue felt a spark of intelligence. Suddenly she was lifting her head and pinning the disgraced master with her stare. "We are all commanded to wear this?"

He nodded, his chin dipping with a firm, angry motion.

"But does the emperor say where we are to display the sign of his generosity?"

Bo Tao's lips curved in a slow smile. "I, too, have been punished," he said firmly, "for you virgins were in my care. I am punished for allowing such a heinous event in the first place. And so it is with great honor and humility that I wear my mark of shame here." Then to everyone's shock, he unbuttoned the top of his jacket. He pulled back the flap of his shirt so that all could see the pinned ribbon resting on the inside of his coat. Then he slowly closed his shirt. If he had not shown it to them, none would have known it was there. Which meant that the tainted virgins could do the same. They could hide their ribbons and have nearly the same chance as everyone else! After all, the Son of Heaven had only seen them during one banquet. How would he tell one virgin apart from another except by a hidden token?

"You arranged this, didn't you, Sun Bo Tao?" Ji Yue asked.

He arched his eyebrow. "The emperor commanded such tokens of shame. Is it my fault that in his fury he forgot to specify the details?"

She smiled, her first real smile of the day. "You risk much in doing this."

He shrugged. "Can I fall further from grace?"

Yes. Yes, he had a great deal further to fall, but he had done it anyway. Ji Yue was the first to step forward, lifting the ugly ornament from his hand. "Thank you, Master of the Festival," she said, her heart in her eyes.

One by one, the other virgins stepped forward, taking their ribbon and secreting it away. "Thank you, Master of the Festival," they murmured, and then disappeared from the main room, their voices raised with renewed excitement.

"You have given them hope for tomorrow," Ji Yue said when it was only the two of them left. There wasn't even a eunuch to guard them, so far had they fallen from grace.

"I would give more," he said as he crossed to stand before her. "I would give you—"

She pressed her hand to his mouth. She did not want to hear his words. She did not want to allow herself to hope. "Tell me truthfully, Sun Bo Tao," she said. "For this shame, what is your punishment?"

He frowned and slowly pulled her hand from his mouth, but he did not release her fingers. "Men are never to blame," he said softly, "even when it is completely our fault." His eyes told her that he blamed himself for everything. For not knowing about the party, for seducing her when she had been all too willing, for everything that had passed. "I am commanded to wear this silly token, and another will speak in my stead at the marriage festival."

So no real punishment. "And afterward?"

He looked down at their intertwined hands. "The position of my choice. I told him I must have an official place of power in his government or I would leave."

She looked up at him, truly pleased. "That is excellent news! Then you can have your own home and take a wife and…" Her voice trailed away. She did not like to think of him taking a wife other than her.

"I would still give it up for you," he said. "We can still run."

She closed her eyes, fighting the urge to rush into his arms. "How would we live?" she asked. "What would you do?" There were no jobs in China for a disgraced man. And that was assuming they were not caught and killed for their audacity.

Bo Tao shrugged. "I could learn something new. Ji Yue, it is not impossible to begin again. There is a very large world outside of China."

"But your whole life has been here. You were born to stand by the emperor's side." Before he could dismiss her objection, she rushed ahead to her next point. "Have you ever been poor?"

"My family is not wealthy, Ji Yue."

"But you grew up here, running with the future Son of Heaven. Have you ever wanted for rice in your bowl?"

"I do not care."

"You will," she returned.

"No, Ji Yue, I won't. Not if you are by my side."

She wanted to believe him. She did believe him. But he belonged in the Forbidden City helping the emperor direct China. She would not let him throw his entire life away just for her. "I care," she said. "I will not run."

He grimaced and made a sound of disgust. "You women are taught sacrifice from the cradle. You are here to serve men, to devote yourself to honor and care for us." He abruptly gripped her arms and roughly hauled her forward. His eyes burned like fire and she gasped in stunned shock. "Even you," he rasped, "with all your intelligence and your fire, you do not think that I need you, Ji Yue. That without you, I will—" he swallowed "—I will be hollow." Then he crushed her mouth to his, kissing her more boldly and passionately than ever before. She melted against him. How she ached for the dream that he offered!

Then he released her. The separation was as abrupt as the kiss, and she swayed on her feet. She wished he would steady her. She wanted to be in his arms again. But he held himself apart, and she was forced to balance herself while his attitude shifted to one of bitter cold.

"Bo Tao—"

"Take these, Ji Yue," he said.

She looked down and saw that he held out two carved jade combs. The one was a dragon coiling in exquisite majesty. The other was a tigress, regal and fierce. Male dragon, female tigress—symbols as old as China—and he was giving them to her. "Why?"

"They were my aunt's. She wore them when she was selected by the last emperor, so she believed them to be lucky. According to her, when the two are separate like this, then the wearer still searches for her true heart. If a man were to steal the dragon from you—" He plucked the dragon comb away from her fingers. "Then he has taken your heart and you belong to him."

Her eyes watered at the sight of him holding the dragon comb tucked against his chest.

"But if you wear them linked like this," he continued, "then you have already found your heart." He reached out and carefully joined the two combs. The mechanism was subtle and intricate, but when he was done, she saw a dragon and tigress locked together in…

She smiled. "That is not an appropriate comb for a virgin."

He shrugged, but his eyes remained serious. "Tomorrow morning the virgins will assemble. They will be placed throughout the gardens and the walkways of the Forbidden City."

"I know."

"The emperor will walk among you and choose one to be his empress, four more to be his primary wives, and the rest will be separated into the middle and lower harems."

She nodded. "Yes, I know."

He pressed the linked combs into her hands. "Wear this comb like this, and the emperor will know your heart is given to another." He took a breath as he carefully separated the two pieces. "Wear them apart and…"

She lifted her head. "And what?"

"And I believe he will select you as his empress."

"What?" she gasped. The shock of his statement set her heart to clamoring in her throat.

His lips twisted into a rueful grimace. "Do you not understand why I was made master of the festival? Do you not know my strengths even now?"

She knew his intelligence and his compassion. She knew his fierce passion for his country and his virility as a man. "Which strength?" she laughed. "There are so many."

He flashed a smile at her, but then it disappeared. "Yi Zhen set me the task of finding the most perfect of the virgins, the smartest and the most wholesome." He released a short breath. "He wanted me to find the best woman to be empress. And I found her."

"Me?" she breathed.

"You."

She shook her head, the whole conversation overwhelming. "But will he listen to you? He would pick me as his empress?"

"I believe so, yes. If you leave the combs apart, he will know that you offer yourself to him and to China."

She swallowed. It was an awesome destiny and the very dream she had set for herself when she'd first learned of the festival. "And if I link the combs, Bo Tao, what then? What is to happen to me then?" She searched his face for the truth, but saw only uncertainty.

"I cannot say, Ji Yue. I have asked for a boon. I have pleaded for my wishes, but…" He paused as he looked down at their joined hands.

"Was he terribly angry with you?" she whispered.

He released a short laugh. "It is a terrible thing to steal a woman from your best friend."

"Especially if that man is the emperor of China."

"Exactly so."

There was a noise in the hallway. Two girls chattering with an excitement that had not been present in the palace since the tainted virgins arrived. Bo Tao sent her a desperate look, then stepped away from her. She was left holding the two combs—one in each hand.

"I cannot promise anything, Ji Yue. I can only hope."

She would have said something then, except she did not know how to respond. And then their time together was lost. The girls came around the corner, gasping in surprise when they saw the disgraced master still standing there.

Bo Tao arched his brow at them, silently daring them to question his presence. They flushed bright red, then scurried away. Bo Tao looked at her, but she shook her head. He could not risk speaking plainly again. Where one virgin lurked, whispering and giggling in gossip, a dozen more were sure to follow.

He understood her message and knew it to be true. So he gave her the deepest bow she had ever received, then turned and walked away.

20

JI YUE'S FEET ACHED, her back had tightened into a knot of anxiety and her head felt as if it weighed a ton. She stood in the back of the Festival Garden, waiting with all the other virgins for the emperor to wander by and make his selection. If only she could move a little, wander the gardens and ease the aches in her body, but she was too terrified to move.

She was being ridiculous, she knew. Only an idiot would believe that the emperor would miss her just because she took a step or two in a different direction. But she had been told to stand here, that the emperor would wander through eventually, and so here she stood. At least she had a position where she could see some of the path. Li Fei fidgeted just a little ahead of her around a curve, but Ji Yue had been placed here— no doubt by the dowager consort—in the furthest reaches of the garden. The shrew probably hoped that the emperor would select his primary harem long before he made it to her.

Fortunately, Ji Yue had Bo Tao's assurance that the emperor would find her and that he planned on selecting her as empress. She fretted because she didn't know what she would tell the emperor when he finally did wander back here to talk. She held her two combs in her hands, alternately linking them together and snapping them apart. If she wasn't careful, she'd soon break the delicate mechanism.

Linked combs meant her heart was already given to someone else, to Bo Tao. Separate combs said she wanted desperately for the emperor to select her. A fairly simple choice, really: become an empress or a woman on the run with a disgraced husband.

But even with such clear choice, she didn't know what to do. A night's tormented sleep had shown her just how much she loved Bo Tao. She longed to see his face, to touch his cheek, to feel his arms tenderly tuck her close to his side. She loved everything about him and would willingly give her life if it somehow saved him.

Unfortunately, the only way she could "save" him would be to *not* marry him. Without her, he still had a political career. Even if the emperor forgave Bo Tao for seducing an imperial virgin, he was not likely to reward such behavior. He certainly wouldn't want Bo Tao around. But if Ji Yue chose the emperor, then Bo Tao would get the political position of his choice. With that, he could marry, have children and still live the life he was born to lead.

Meanwhile, she had been raised from birth to be a political wife. She had watched her mother guide her father's career. A smart woman could do much even from behind the women's screen. Ji Yue could be an enormous asset to any man, but the emperor himself? That was the kind of influence that was her mother's dream. Up until a few days ago, that had been her own dream, as well. But then Bo Tao had slipped into her palanquin and everything had changed.

She stared at the linked combs in her hands and forced herself to break them apart. Every shred of reason she possessed screamed that she should become the empress. The best way to help the man she loved was to give him up. The best thing for her family was to become empress. And the best way for her to do the work she wanted—to help a great husband in a political career—would be to humbly accept her role as empress of China. She had to marry the emperor. She *wanted* to marry the emperor.

Except, of course, she did not. She wanted Bo Tao. And the next time she looked down at her hands, the combs were once again linked. No matter what logic said, clearly her heart wanted Bo Tao.

She had just forced herself to separate the combs—again— when she heard a rustle ahead on the path. Was it the emperor? Or were the virgins getting tired and moving around? It was so hard to see! Then she heard voices. A man's voice, but it could be a eunuch. A female giggle—definitely a virgin's, given how nervous it sounded—and then more rustling. The anxiety was killing her!

She heard a voice. The dowager consort! "There's nothing interesting back there," she said, probably to her son. "The other girls are up here."

The pronouncement was seconded by the head eunuch. Then there was much bustling and movement while Ji Yue looked down in defeat. It didn't matter if she linked or unlinked her combs. The emperor would never be given the chance to wander back here. His mother was head of the women in the Forbidden City and—

"You must be Chen Ji Yue."

Ji Yue started, looking up in shock as the emperor sauntered down the path. She'd thought…well, it didn't matter what she thought, since he was here now! She sank low, starting her kowtow, but he reached out and stopped her.

"Yes, yes, but let me see your face," he said. He physically pulled her upright, scanning her face as if trying to place her in his memory. Meanwhile, she looked from his hand on her arm, up his impressive imperial tunic and finally to his rather ordinary face. Was this man to be her husband? This man trailed by his mother and a score of eunuchs? This man who did *not* give her shivers or make her heart lurch in her chest? And would she always, always compare him to Bo Tao?

Meanwhile the emperor had ceased studying her face to look down at the combs in her hand. Unfortunately, she had been in the process of linking them. Or unlinking them. She didn't even remember now! They were half-intertwined and that was no clear message at all.

"You seem to have dropped your combs, Chen Ji Yue."

Had he emphasized two combs? Not one? "Yes," she murmured, beginning to hold them up for his inspection. *Separate them! Become the empress!* she ordered her hands. She began to do it, but then paused, finding a boldness that came from irritation. Second-guessing herself was getting her nowhere. She needed to ask exactly what she wanted to know. So she did.

"Do you remember me, Emperor?"

He smiled in a vague way. "Of course, of course. Your beauty makes an impression."

She arched her brows at him. "That and what I said at the celebration."

He frowned and then his expression abruptly cleared as memory sparked. "Oh, yes. About peasants and servants. That impressed Bo Tao." But obviously not the emperor. His gaze wandered across the gardens to the girls stretching and contorting themselves around corners to catch his eye. "I suppose whatever it takes to distinguish one of you from the other. And you must be well able to manage servants. A valuable asset in an empress."

He reached for her comb to take the dragon piece from her.

This was the moment. If she let him take it from her, then she would become an empress and spend her life…doing what? Managing his servants. He had no appreciation of the skills she brought to his side. He would never allow her to hide in the shadows of the women's screen to take notes. Neither would he bring his cares to her at night to help him sort through one difficult problem or another.

The emperor was a man who relied not on his wives, but on his assistants. On men like Bo Tao, who would recommend policy and select his wives. It would be a near impossible task to get him to see her as anything but a baby-making vessel. And what a miserable life that would be!

She couldn't do it. She couldn't be that kind of woman to him. So with tears of regret in her eyes, she pulled the combs away from the emperor. "I am so clumsy with this," she said as she quickly linked them together. "They are supposed to be one comb, and they go—"

"No, Chen Ji Yue," he interrupted, his expression hard. "No, they are two combs, and I believe this one is mine."

She stared at him in shock as he forced the linked combs out of her hands. With a quick twist, he released the catch, then dropped the dragon comb into an inside pocket. The tigress comb was offered back to her.

"B-but, Emperor," she stammered. Then she lifted her chin and pointed. "Did you see Li Fei? She will do everything you want. And she will never talk to you of…of servants or peasants. Ever."

He craned his neck a bit to see where she pointed. "Hmm," he murmured. "Li Fei?"

She nodded, and as she watched, he waved a negligent hand at a eunuch then started moving on. Ji Yue wanted to follow him. She wanted to run after the man and demand her comb back. How could he just take it? And now Bo Tao would think that she had selected power over him, that she wanted the emperor of China over him. And it just wasn't true!

But it was too late. As soon as the emperor moved on, scores of eunuchs scurried directly behind. Between one breath and the next, she was completely cut off. And now the emperor had her comb! If Bo Tao was right, she was about to become the next empress of China, but it wasn't the choice she wanted!

She stood there helplessly watching the backs of all the people who trailed her future husband. But he was already gone, well beyond her reach or influence.

She began to cry.

THE SELECTION WAS COMPLETE. All the virgins were assembled in the main palace to hear the results. The virgins would be separated, the newest empress revered.

Ji Yue waited, her heart skipping and tripping inside her chest. One moment she was elated at the idea of taking her place beside the emperor of China. The next she craned her neck to see Bo Tao, to silently tell him that this was not her choice, that she had chosen him. But as a disgraced master of the festival, he was nowhere to be found.

She remembered how little use she would be as empress: watched on every side, in constant battle with the dowager consort and completely ignored by her husband. At that moment her mood crashed downward in despair. Why had she ever wanted such a ridiculous thing? This was insane!

But then the excitement of the moment, the ceremony and the majesty of the palace filtered into her thoughts again, and her spirit quivered in excitement. Empress of China! Her mother would be so excited! Her brothers and father would have no need to worry ever again!

The moment of glory was at hand. The new master of the festival stood before the Dragon Throne, a scroll in his hands, and he began to call their names. This girl—middle harem. Hua Si, her evil roommate—lowest harem. Li Fei—favored concubine. Li Fei was one of the four favored women! Ji Yue was happy; she looked forward to having a friend so close to her.

Then Ji Yue was called. The sound of her name echoed through the palace walls and sent a thrill down her spine. Soon she would be Empress Ji Yue. Her hands were shaking, her mouth was dry, but she was prepared.

"Lowest harem!"

Ji Yue blinked. She couldn't possibly have heard correctly. She was supposed to be first wife. Empress! She stood there stupidly staring at the Dragon Throne. It could not be true. But hands grabbed her arm and roughly dragged her aside to the place for the lowest and most forgotten harem. She was pushed next to Hua Si. And as she stood there, she still could not comprehend what had happened.

She was not going to be empress? But Bo Tao had said! And at the thought of him, more realities came crashing down. Not only was she not going to be empress, she was not going to be with Bo Tao, either. She was, however, going to be tormented and reviled by the dowager consort, head eunuch and Hua Si, as well! For the rest of her life!

It was all she could do not to scream and plunge a knife into her chest.

21

Ji Yue was dressed for pleasure. Against all odds, she of the lowest harem had been selected for this night. The official wedding wouldn't be for many days yet. There were rituals to observe and celestial timing to ensure the most auspicious union of man and woman, emperor and empress.

But for tonight, the emperor called for a woman. As she was of the lowest harem, the date of her actual wedding to the emperor was of little consequence. In short, tonight she was called, and tonight she would sleep with the emperor. If she was blessed, her womb would be fruitful and she would bear the emperor a son, who would then be taken from her and given to the empress to raise as her child. Such was the lot of the women in the lowest harem.

If she were truly blessed, the emperor would do his business with her and then leave without noticing her state of virginity. The doctor had inserted medicine into her womb to make it tight. But if that was not enough, Ji Yue had also hidden a small knife in the bodice of her gown. It would be easy to make a nick in her skin somewhere unseen and then smear the blood where it was needed. Assuming, of course, that the knife was at hand and the emperor did not notice what she was doing.

And so Ji Yue was dressed according to the dictates of the

eunuchs. Her gown was of the lightest silk, her hair twisted and coiled, but held in place by her tigress comb. That had been explicitly ordered by someone, presumably the emperor. Then she was escorted with minimal pomp to the emperor's palace and ordered to climb into his massive bed. She was even instructed on the appropriate words to say to her new husband about how great an honor it was to serve him, how she gloried at his merest touch. On and on the list went until she thought she would scream at the repetition of it.

And then, as the time neared, the instructional eunuchs withdrew. She lay in the massive bed and worried about what to do. She knew this was a great honor and a great opportunity. If she pleased the emperor tonight, he might lift her out of the lowest harem into a more powerful position. She ought to be thinking of ways to seduce him. And yet, try as she might, she could not help but think of Bo Tao. How wonderful it would be to lie in anticipation of a night with him. How she would delight to wake in his arms tomorrow, to bear his child in the days to come. How she wished...

A noise disturbed her thoughts and she froze like a terrified rabbit. The emperor was coming! He entered the bedchamber The soft light of the lanterns seemed to accentuate his face and his physique rather than the exquisite embroidery on the black silk of his robe. Ji Yue pushed herself upright in bed as she tamped down any comparisons between the emperor and Bo Tao. Clearly, the emperor did not practice his physical skills as much as Bo Tao. He was not as muscular nor as powerful, in a purely physical sense. But he was her husband and her emperor, and so she tried to smile invitingly at him. He paused near the bed, looking down at her. Then he abruptly burst into laughter.

"I have never seen a more reluctant woman," he boomed.

Ji Yue blanched and mentally scrambled for something clever to say. All she could come up with was one of her prescribed phrases. "I glory to share my body with your magnificence."

"Except you look like you'd rather be eating cow dung."

She opened her mouth, but no sound came out. How could she save this disaster?

"But am I not magnificent, Chen Ji Yue? Every woman's desire?" The emperor threw his arms wide and let the folds of his robe gape open over his chest. It was a pale chest, and not very wide—or at least not as wide as Bo Tao's. She tried to summon an adoring look.

"I am overcome with your glory," she said, trying to put passion into her words.

The emperor dropped his arms and huffed in disgust. "You really are in love, aren't you?"

She had no idea what to say to that. Did she lie? He hadn't believed anything she'd said so far. At her silence, he drew out the dragon comb.

"According to legend, he who holds this comb is the true mate to the woman who wears the tigress." He gestured to the carved comb still in her hair.

She swallowed and touched the tigress. "Is that the legend?" she asked, her voice trembling.

The emperor shrugged and released another laugh. "I have no idea. It's just some nonsense Bo Tao told me." Then he waggled it in front of her eyes. "But I have it, so you must therefore adore me!"

She blinked and tried to nod, but she was terribly frightened. What was she supposed to do when the emperor of China acted like a lunatic! Was he playing some devious game? She didn't understand!

"Oops!" he cried as the comb slipped from his fingers to the floor. "I have dropped it." Then he stood there with his hands on his hips, clearly waiting, but for what? Did he want her to pick it up? There was no one else in the room, so it would have to be her. She began to climb out of bed, but he threw out a hand to stop her.

"Not you!" he snapped. Then he abruptly clapped his hands. "Come in here, you fool! I have dropped my comb!"

Did he address someone else in the room? She thought they were alone. And yet, people were always close in the Forbidden City. Within moments, a eunuch came scurrying in to retrieve the fallen comb. Except this eunuch did not move like any that she had seen so far. In fact, Ji Yue thought as she narrowed her eyes, this eunuch looked extraordinarily familiar.

Bo Tao! She gasped and scrambled onto her knees. It was all she dared with the emperor looming over her.

"You called?" her love said, but the emperor cut him off.

"I have dropped my comb. Pick it up for me, Bo Tao."

Her love clenched his jaw, and his gaze darted between the emperor and Ji Yue. She wanted to say something to him. She wanted to tell him that the leader of China was an extremely bizarre man. She needed to tell him that she had never willingly given the emperor the comb. He had stolen it and her heart belonged to Bo Tao. But she couldn't say those things, and so she watched in miserable silence as Bo Tao slowly bent down and retrieved the dragon comb. Then he straightened, his face an emotionless mask as he held it out to the emperor.

But Yi Zhen didn't take it. Instead, he snatched the tigress comb out of her hair. She squeaked in alarm. After all, he had grabbed a few strands of hair, too. While both she and Bo Tao watched in confusion, the emperor quickly linked the two pieces together and turned to her.

"Do you think, Chen Ji Yue, that the emperor of China is a god who can rule men's hearts?"

She swallowed, wondering what he could possibly mean. "I believe that you are a man who leads China and so gains the love of the people you rule."

The emperor huffed. "So, not a god, then? But I am the Son of Heaven!"

She dipped her head. "You live in our hearts, nonetheless."

"Your friend Li Fei said I was a god. She said she worshiped me."

Ji Yue grimaced. That sounded exactly like something Li Fei would say.

"You are right," the emperor finally said. "I like her better. Which means," he said with a flourish, "that I have no use for you." He turned to Bo Tao. "Which means I can gift her to you. By my hand and—" he passed the linked combs to Bo Tao "—this silly trinket, I declare you two wed." Then his gaze softened. "Enjoy her, my friend. As for me, I prefer to be a god to the women I bed." And with that, he laughed heartily at Bo Tao's stunned expression.

"Yi Zhen," he began, his voice choked.

"Yes, yes, I know. You worship me. You think I am a god. You forget that you are supposed to call me Emperor Xian Feng."

"Emper—"

"Hss! Come to me in the morning and we will discuss your exact appointment."

"B-but—" Bo Tao stammered again.

"Fine, fine. The afternoon then."

"Yi Zhen—"

"Oh, and you!" The emperor spun around and pinned her

with a cold stare. "If ever he falters in his devotion to me, then I will send for you. I will recall you to my harem, and it will not go well for you."

Ji Yue nodded, her mind reeling. Could it be possible? Could she now be wed to Bo Tao?

"So take her!" the emperor ordered as he clapped his friend on the back.

Bo Tao dropped to the floor in a kowtow. Ji Yue scrambled to do the same, her shock and her gratitude overwhelming her. They both pressed their foreheads to the ground four times. Five times. But by the sixth, they raised themselves up and discovered they were alone. Together.

Ji Yue looked into Bo Tao's eyes. She saw so many emotions there, so many conflicting thoughts. She understood because she felt the same.

"The emperor is very odd," she whispered, though that was not at all what she wanted to say.

"It is hard to rule a country. He takes his pleasure however he can."

"I did not give him the comb, Bo Tao. I held them linked together but he broke them apart. He took it from me."

Bo Tao's eyes lighted in surprise and hope. "You chose me? Over being an empress?"

She nodded. "I love you. I could not—" She didn't get any more words out. He kissed her. He pulled her into his arms and kissed her as she had dreamed. He kissed her and he did not stop for a long, incredible time.

It wasn't until she welcomed him joyfully into her body that he spoke again. "I love you," he said. "I will not be separated from you ever again."

"Never," she echoed as she wrapped her legs around him and another dance began.

Hours later, they watched the dawn together. They lay intertwined and whispered secrets to each other. They made plans and spoke of love. And so began a most glorious union in the bed of the emperor of China.

Epilogue

"WHERE IS THAT WASTREL MAN who destroyed you?"

Mama's voice boomed through their home, and Ji Yue looked up at her husband with horror in her eyes. They'd been married barely two days and had only just left the Forbidden City with all the pomp the emperor could give. Her parents had been at the ceremony, of course, her mother smiling and nodding with her customary aplomb, but Mama's eyes had been cold whenever she looked at her daughter. And now, a day later, she was at their new home and the reckoning was at hand.

"Don't worry, my love," Bo Tao said. "I will handle your mother."

"You don't know what she's like—"

"Ji Yue! Where are you?"

Ji Yue sighed and stood. "We are in the library, Mama." She stepped around the women's screen and opened the door. Mama stomped down the hallway to her, and Ji Yue forced herself to smile warmly, though inside her heart quivered in fear. Mama did not look happy.

"You!" Mama bellowed, completely ignoring her daughter to glare at her new son-in-law. "I know your worth, Sun Bo Tao, and I spit upon it! But for you my daughter would be an empress!"

"Mama!" Ji Yue cried, but Bo Tao held up his hand to stop her. Then he turned his smile on his new mother-in-law and gestured to a nearby chair.

"Would you like some tea?"

"I want nothing from you who ruined—"

"Good, then. That means we will finish by the time the English ambassador gets here."

Mama frowned as she peered out the window toward the street. "The white devil comes here?"

Ji Yue stepped forward. "The head white devil, Mama. Bo Tao has been named first minister to the Dragon Throne. His salary is commensurate with a general." Ji Yue gestured to the area behind the screen. It was tight in this little room, but there was adequate space for her desk. "I will sit here and take notes."

Mama's inked-in eyebrows shot up to her hairline. "He lets you take notes on his meetings?"

"I begged her to do it," he said. "She is brilliant in her notes. You taught her well."

Mama nodded, accepting her due. "She would have been an excellent empress."

"In that," Bo Tao said with a bite in his tone, "you did not teach her well." Mama gasped in shock, but Bo Tao did not give her time to speak. "You taught her that she is smart—"

"She is smart!"

"She is brilliant," Bo Tao agreed. "But you also said she was not beautiful." Then he stepped forward. "Do you know nothing about men, Madame Chen? Her skin glows, her smile is alluring, her waist is willowy and seductive."

Mama grimaced. "Aie, I have taught her to hide her flaws."

"There are no flaws, Madame Chen. Her feet are beautiful, and her smile lights the heavens. Had she known these things, she might indeed have caught the emperor's eye. But you missed her beauty, and so she had no understanding of her true worth."

Mama stood, flabbergasted by Bo Tao's criticism. It was the first time that Ji Yue had seen her mother with her mouth hanging open. And in that silence, her new husband continued.

"I saw your daughter's worth immediately, her beauty, her charm and, yes, her brilliance, and I wanted her for myself."

"You admit it then!"

He bowed. "Of course. Because I am a man who sees worth even the emperor does not. That is why I am now first minister." He went and drew Ji Yue into his arms. "I see my wife's value. I know that she is perfect in every way." Then he leaned forward. "Just as I see your value, Madame Chen."

Mama straightened, and her eyes narrowed. "What do you mean?"

"One wife who listens behind the women's screen, who speaks to the visitors' wives and hears the chatter of children is invaluable. But to have two women—one young and beautiful, the other canny in the ways of the older generation—that would be a treasure beyond compare."

Mama paused, her brow furrowed in thought. "I serve my husband," she said slowly.

"Of course," Bo Tao agreed with a smile. "I would expect nothing less, especially since your husband's fame will grow when it is known that his daughter is wife to the first minister." He turned and pressed a warm kiss to Ji Yue's forehead. "But in our new house, there will be a much larger library with more room behind the women's screen. And I will have work enough for many assistants."

"You would allow me to listen!" gasped Mama. "To serve the first minister even though I am a woman?"

He laughed, the sound full and hearty. "I see worth where

the emperor merely sees breasts and a womb. Do you wish to work, Madame Chen? Do you wish to help your daughter and son-in-law?"

Mama didn't answer in words, but her eyes shone with hope and gratitude.

"Do not stint your husband," he continued. "And I will hear no insults to my wife!"

"I would not dream of such a thing!"

"The women's area in our home is under Ji Yue's charge. I will not gainsay her."

Mama nodded vigorously. "As is right and proper for a good husband."

"Then we are agreed?" Bo Tao asked. "My wife is perfect in every way?"

Mama bowed her head. "My daughter is most fortunate in her husband."

Bo Tao laughed as he pulled Ji Yue closer. "I am the fortunate one." He glanced nervously at the street. "The ambassador will be here soon. You must go now," he said to his mother-in-law. "There is not room behind the screen for more than one."

Mama nodded. "I will leave immediately," she said as she rushed away.

Ji Yue watched her mother depart, amazement in her heart. "You have given her new life, new purpose. Papa's career could never adequately use her talents."

"I meant what I said," Bo Tao murmured as he twisted her to rest flush against his body.

"Yes," she murmured, growing more distracted by the minute. "Mama will make an excellent assistant."

Bo Tao pulled her face to his. "I meant what I said about you. You are beautiful and brilliant, and I am the most fortunate of husbands."

Warmth flooded her heart. "I love you," she said as she pressed her lips to his.

"And I love you," he answered. "Plus, I am the most fortunate of husbands for another reason entirely."

"Oh?" she asked as he pushed her backward against the wall.

"The English ambassador is not due for another hour."

She giggled as her husband began to touch her in ways that only he knew, taking her to places they could only find together. Then, just before she completely surrendered to his caress, she realized something enormous.

She had won! She wasn't empress of China, but she had won something much more important: the love of a good man. And that, she decided was a far, far better prize.

* * * * *

*Harlequin is 60 years old,
and Harlequin Blaze is celebrating!
After all, a lot can happen in 60 years,
or 60 minutes…or 60 seconds!
Find out what's going down in
Blaze's heart-stopping new miniseries,
FROM 0 TO 60!
Getting from "Hello" to "How was it?
can happen fast….*

*Here's a sneak peek of the first book,
A LONG, HARD RIDE
by Alison Kent
Available March 2009.*

"Is that for me?" Trey asked.

Cardin Worth cocked her head to the side and considered how much better the day already seemed. "Good morning to you, too."

When she didn't hold out the second cup of coffee for him to take, he came closer. She sipped from her heavy white mug, hiding her grin and her giddy rush of nerves behind it.

But when he stopped in front of her, she made the mistake of lowering her gaze from his face to the exposed strip of his chest. It was either give him his cup of coffee or bury her nose against him and breathe in. She remembered so clearly how he smelled. How he tasted.

She gave him his coffee.

After taking a quick gulp, he smiled and said, "Good morning, Cardin. I hope the floor wasn't too hard for you."

The hardness of the floor hadn't been the problem. She shook her head. "Are you kidding? I slept like a baby, swaddled in my sleeping bag."

"In my sleeping bag, you mean."

If he wanted to get technical, yeah. "Thanks for the loaner. It made sleeping on the floor almost bearable." As had the warmth of his spooned body, she thought, then quickly changed the subject. "I saw you have a loaf of bread and some eggs. Would you like me to cook breakfast?"

He lowered his coffee mug slowly, his gaze as warm as the

sun on her shoulders, as the ceramic heating her hands. "I didn't bring you out here to wait on me."

"You didn't bring me out here at all. I volunteered to come."

"To help me get ready for the race. Not to serve me."

"It's just breakfast, Trey. And coffee." Even if last night it had been more. Even if the way he was looking at her made her want to climb back into that sleeping bag. "I work much better when my stomach's not growling. I thought it might be the same for you."

"It is, but I'll cook. You made the coffee."

"That's because I can't work at all without caffeine."

"If I'd known that, I would've put on a pot as soon I got up."

"What time *did* you get up?" Judging by the sun's position, she swore it couldn't be any later than seven now. And, yeah, they'd agreed to start working at six.

"Maybe four?" he guessed, giving her a lazy smile.

"But it was almost two…" She let the sentence dangle, finishing the thought privately. She was quite sure he knew exactly what time they'd finally fallen asleep after he'd made love to her.

The question facing her now was where did this relationship—if you could even call it *that*—go from here?

* * * * *

Cardin and Trey are about to find out that great sex
is only the beginning….
Don't miss the fireworks!
Get ready for
A LONG, HARD RIDE
by Alison Kent
Available March 2009,
wherever Blaze books are sold.

CELEBRATE
60 YEARS
OF PURE READING PLEASURE
WITH HARLEQUIN®!

**We'll be spotlighting a different series
every month throughout 2009
to celebrate our 60th anniversary.**

Look for Harlequin® Blaze™ in March!

0-60

*After all, a lot can happen in 60 years,
or 60 minutes...or 60 seconds!*

Find out what's going down in Blaze's
heart-stopping new miniseries *0-60!*
Getting from "Hello" to "How was it?"
can happen fast....

Look for the brand-new 0-60 miniseries in March 2009!

www.eHarlequin.com   HBRIDE09

DIAMOND IN THE ROUGH

John Callister is a millionaire rancher, yet when he meets lovely Sassy Peale and she thinks he's a cowboy, he goes along with her misconception. He's had enough of gold diggers, and this is a chance to be valued for himself, not his money. But when Sassy finds out the truth, she feels John was merely playing with her. John will have to convince her that he's truly the man she fell in love with—a diamond in the rough.

THE MEN OF MEDICINE RIDGE—a brand-new miniseries set in the wilds of Montana!

Available April 2009 wherever you buy books.

HARLEQUIN® *Romance*®

This February the Harlequin® Romance series
will feature six Diamond Brides stories featuring
diamond proposals and gorgeous grooms.

Share your dream wedding proposal and you could WIN!

The most romantic entry will win a diamond
necklace and will inspire a proposal in one of
our upcoming Diamond Grooms books in 2010.

In 100 words or less, tell us the most romantic
way that you dream of being proposed to.

For more information, and to enter
the Diamond Brides Proposal contest, please visit
www.DiamondBridesProposal.com

Or mail your entry to us at:
IN THE U.S.: 3010 Walden Ave., P.O. Box 9069, Buffalo, NY 14269-9069
IN CANADA: 225 Duncan Mill Road, Don Mills, ON M3B 3K9

REQUEST YOUR FREE BOOKS!

2 FREE NOVELS PLUS 2 FREE GIFTS!

HARLEQUIN®

Blaze™

Red-hot reads!

YES! Please send me 2 FREE Harlequin® Blaze™ novels and my 2 FREE gifts (gifts are worth about $10). After receiving them, if I don't wish to receive any more books, I can return the shipping statement marked "cancel". If I don't cancel, I will receive 6 brand-new novels every month and be billed just $4.24 per book in the U.S. or $4.71 per book in Canada, plus 25¢ shipping and handling per book and applicable taxes, if any*. That's a savings of 15% or more off the cover price! I understand that accepting the 2 free books and gifts places me under no obligation to buy anything. I can always return a shipment and cancel at any time. Even if I never buy another book, the two free books and gifts are mine to keep forever.

151 HDN ERVA 351 HDN ERUX

Name	(PLEASE PRINT)	
Address		Apt. #
City	State/Prov.	Zip/Postal Code

Signature (if under 18, a parent or guardian must sign)

Mail to the **Harlequin Reader Service:**
IN U.S.A.: P.O. Box 1867, Buffalo, NY 14240-1867
IN CANADA: P.O. Box 609, Fort Erie, Ontario L2A 5X3

Not valid to current subscribers of Harlequin Blaze books.

Want to try two free books from another line?
Call 1-800-873-8635 or visit www.morefreebooks.com.

* Terms and prices subject to change without notice. N.Y. residents add applicable sales tax. Canadian residents will be charged applicable provincial taxes and GST. Offer not valid in Quebec. This offer is limited to one order per household. All orders subject to approval. Credit or debit balances in a customer's account(s) may be offset by any other outstanding balance owed by or to the customer. Please allow 4 to 6 weeks for delivery. Offer available while quantities last.

Your Privacy: Harlequin Books is committed to protecting your privacy. Our Privacy Policy is available online at www.eHarlequin.com or upon request from the Reader Service. From time to time we make our lists of customers available to reputable third parties who may have a product or service of interest to you. If you would prefer we not share your name and address, please check here. ☐

HB08R

nocturne™

USA TODAY bestselling author

MAUREEN CHILD

VANISHED

Guardians

Immortal Guardian Rogan Butler
had no use for love, especially after his
Destined Mate abandoned him. So when beautiful
mortal Allison Blair sought his help against a
rising evil force, Rogan was bewildered by the
undeniable electric connection between them.
Besides, his true love had died years ago,
and it was impossible that he could even
have another Destined Mate—wasn't it?

Available February 2009 wherever books are sold.

www.eHarlequin.com
www.paranormalromanceblog.wordpress.com   SN61804

The Inside Romance newsletter has a NEW look for the new year!

Same great content, brand-new look!

The Inside Romance newsletter is a FREE quarterly newsletter highlighting our upcoming series releases and promotions!

Click on the Inside Romance link on the front page of **www.eHarlequin.com** or e-mail us at insideromance@harlequin.ca to sign up to receive your FREE newsletter today!

You can also subscribe by writing to us at: HARLEQUIN BOOKS Attention: Customer Service Department P.O. Box 9057, Buffalo, NY 14269-9057

Please allow 4-6 weeks for delivery of the first issue by mail.

IRNNEW09

You're invited to join our Tell Harlequin Reader Panel!

By joining our new reader panel you will:

- Receive Harlequin® books—they are FREE and yours to keep with no obligation to purchase anything!
- Participate in fun online surveys
- Exchange opinions and ideas with women just like you
- Have a say in our new book ideas and help us publish the best in women's fiction

In addition, you will have a chance to win great prizes and receive special gifts! See Web site for details. Some conditions apply. Space is limited.

To join, visit us at
www.TellHarlequin.com.

COMING NEXT MONTH
Available February 10, 2009

#453 A LONG, HARD RIDE Alison Kent
From 0–60
All Cardin Worth wants is to put her broken family together again. And if that means seducing Trey Davis, her first love, well, a girl's got to do what a girl's got to do. Only, she never expected to enjoy it quite so much....

#454 UP CLOSE AND DANGEROUSLY SEXY Karen Anders
Drew Miller's mission: train a fellow agent's twin sister to replace her in a sting op. Expect the unexpected is his mantra, but he never anticipated that his trainee, Allie Carpenter, would be teaching him a thing or twelve in the bedroom!

#455 ONCE AN OUTLAW Debbi Rawlins
Stolen from Time, Bk. 1
Sam Watkins has a past he's trying to forget. Reese Winslow is desperate to remember a way home. Caught in the Old West, they share an intensely passionate affair that has them joining forces. But does that mean they'll be together forever?

#456 STILL IRRESISTIBLE Dawn Atkins
Years ago Callie Cummings and Declan O'Neill had an unforgettable fling. And now she's back in town. He's still tempting, still irresistible, and she can't get images of him and tangled sheets out of her mind. The only solution? An unforgettable fling, round two.

#457 ALWAYS READY Joanne Rock
Uniformly Hot!
Lieutenant Damon Craig has always tried to live up to the Coast Guard motto: Always Ready. But when sexy sociologist Lacey Sutherland stumbles into a stakeout, alerting his suspects—and his libido—Damon knows he doesn't stand a chance....

#458 BODY CHECK Elle Kennedy
When sexually frustrated professor Hayden Houston meets hot hockey star Brody Croft in a bar, she's ready for a one-night stand. But can Brody convince Hayden that he's good for more than just a body check?

www.eHarlequin.com

HBCNMBPA0209